Highways and Dancehalls

Highways and Dancehalls

Diana Atkinson

Alfred A. Knopf Canada

Published by Alfred A. Knopf Canada

First Edition

Canadian Cataloguing in Publication Data
Atkinson, Diana
Highways & dancehalls

ISBN 0-394-28062-8

I. Title.

PS8551.T55H5 1995   C813'.54   C95-930449-5
PR9199.3.A75H5 1995

Printed and bound in the United States of America

Illustrations: Tony Smith
Map: Tom Sankey

The author wishes to thank the Explorations program
of the Canada Council for a grant which assisted in the
completion of this novel.

Also, heartfelt thanks to Louise Dennys and the
other wonderful women of Knopf Canada: Diane Martin,
Kathryn Mulders, Susan Burns, Susan Roxborough,
and Geraldine Quan.

Thank you Kay Lukes, Carole Corbeil,
Caryl Phillips, and Fiona McCrae for encouragement
at earlier stages.

And finally, thank you, Clint Atkinson, for your
thousand kindnesses, your gentle character, and your
tireless interest and devotion.

For Eve

Mountains ⭐
Roads and Highways ---
0   500
Kilometres

Whitehorse **YUKON**
TERRITORY

NORTHWEST
TERRITORIES

USA

Fort Liard

Liard River

BRITISH

Fort Nelson

COLUMBIA

Prince *Terrace*
Rupert
Smithers
Kitimat
Burns Lake

Fort
St. John
Dawson Creek

Prince George

ALBERTA

Port Hardy

Williams Lake

Cache
Creek

Lillooet

Revelstoke

Squamish
Gibsons

Lytton
Vancouver
Vernon
Golden
Calgary

Nanaimo
Ladysmith
Duncan
Victoria

Surrey
Hope
Kelowna

White Rock
Penticton

Castlegar

U. S. A.

Keepers of private notebooks are a different breed altogether, lonely and disconsolate rearrangers of things—anxious malcontents afflicted, apparently at birth, with a presentiment of loss.
—Joan Didion, *Slouching Towards Bethlehem*

Part One

I am "gyrating," as the journalists say whenever they write about strippers. I'd like to say that I can barely hear myself think over the swell of Cantonese and the driving bass beat, but I can hear myself all too well.

Second song. Well, I guess I can't keep this shiny copper jacket on any longer. But the four hundred heads are too close. Surely my scar will be visible under the relentless yellow-green lights ("hepatitis yellow," Meg would have said). On this small, round pill of a stage, I feel like something in a Petri dish. Several of the men crane past me at blond Sherilee with the flawless tummy and tan lines accentuating her unlikely breasts, over on the centre stage. She is naked already.

If I had implants, it wouldn't matter if I got down to, say, a lace-up glove leather corselette—they'd be too busy ogling my enormous tits. Sighing, I rip the velcro harem pants apart and give them some leg.

On all fours now, grinding my ass so the middle-aged businessman who's wandered over can stuff a fiver in my T-bar. Well, good, I'm thinking—I'm worth *something*, Sherilee notwithstanding—and then I just want to disappear. Twenty feet away a blond man with a lean, intelligent face leans against the red-flocked wall. Motionless, watching me. Watching my eyes. He and I are the only two in the room stone-cold sober. ("Who let him in here?" I think indignantly.)

This man unhinges me more than anyone: more than the avid, plump family men in suits devouring my various body parts, now almost completely unwrapped from my copper lamé tiger-woman costume; more than the dentist I think I recognize from my childhood in the University district (picking his teeth with a little silver instrument, his hand cupped over his mouth). Even when I look away, everywhere but at the blond man, I can feel his gaze. Whenever I glance at him he is still there, arms crossed, regarding me with amused curiosity. What are *you* doing here? his eyes say. My intelligence, so steadily mirrored back, makes me feel ridiculous.

As I play with my G-string (cooing at whoever my face

is aimed at, and over my shoulder at whoever is absorbed in my hind end), I try not to think about what my parents' friends' offspring are doing at this moment. (Wheeling prams in upscale neighbourhoods; assistant teaching at Harvard.)

Something has gone wrong. Chairs are scraped back as Mai Tai, the Japanese-Native who'd been cocktail waitressing before her shift on the far stage, is carried out by two elderly waiters who look like they've seen it all. Her G-string, half off, detaches itself and is pocketed by a businessman, who makes a face. A wave of laughter and Cantonese exclaiming. Somebody leans forward and tosses beer on her snatch. I promise myself: as soon as this is over and I am back out on the sidewalk in my jeans and black wool jacket (I will smell the wet asphalt. I will not look at the hookers shivering in the rain on the corner of Granville and Davie), I will erase this night as if it had never been.

I was a lousy waitress. Actually, I never got beyond busgirl so I guess we'll never know how I would've done as a waitress. As a busgirl at Mallard's, I sucked. I was intimidated by the patrons, sipping and chatting, glittering and clinking in their fancy clothes at the big round tables. Also by the waiters and waitresses, suave and sophisticated on the serving floor, foul-mouthed and abrupt in the kitchen. I got used to being cut off and drowned out, but not to being elbowed, shoved and tripped. I spent most of my time trying to hide from everyone, especially the owner, Bob Mallard, and his stylish wife, Yvonne.

Bob had long red hair and a handlebar moustache. He circulated. As the genial host of Mallard's, he could be seen shaking hands at the door—"Nice to have you with us" when they entered, "So glad you could join us" when they left—or pouring wine from a silver trolley, all dashing gestures, a little white towel draped over his forearm. He would catch my eye across the room, where I was clumsily trying to clear salad plates by stacking them in spite of their mounds of lettuce, so that the vinaigrette dripped on to the tablecloth, the carpet, and the suede shoes of the (as yet) oblivious lady diner, in a kind of fountain effect. Seeing his expression, which would miraculously transform from a model of gracious servility to an eye-popping, head-shaking, "No, no, NO!!", I would hastily abandon the plates on the nearest surface—a passing tray of hors-d'oeuvres, say—or drag a filthy bus tub to the tableside, which was enough to put the diners off dessert. Afterwards, I would attempt to melt into the shadows; not easy, in a white blouse.

For as long as I lasted, which was longer than I would have had my boyfriend, Lloyd, not been second cook, Bob and I played cat and mouse. A glimpse of his red whiskers would send me scurrying. If Bob was in the kitchen "having a word with" the cooks ("That cream sauce needs more wine. And the marengo is too salty—someone com-plained"), I huddled at the edge of the serving floor, pol-ishing silver. If he was on the floor, I helped the dish-washer. This was restful. Facing the food-splattered wall in the steamy dish pit, I was less likely to make chance eye contact with anyone, including Yvonne, who was fre-quently head waitress. ("I've been looking for you. Tables 3,5, and 9 have been sitting in dirty dishes for the past fif-teen minutes. And for heaven's sake, do something with your hair!" Pivoting sharply, she'd be gone, leaving me in a cloud of steam in which White Shoulders now mingled with the smell of discarded food.)

If it seemed Bob and Yvonne were everywhere, nat-tering and hissing at me, or if I was on the brink of tears, or both, I hid in the bathroom, where I tried not to look in the mirror. I knew I'd be dismayed at the sight of my face above the rumpled blouse, at the limp curls stuck to my forehead, at my brimming eyes.

"You have no future in the restaurant business," said Bob when he fired me. Sadly, I had to agree.

I met one-eyed Lloyd in the unemployment office soon after I quit high school at seventeen.

He took me back to the warehouse where he was crash-ing. It was bare except for a foam rubber mattress on the floor, a nailed-together table, and a console record player he'd got from the Sally Ann. I was wearing cut-offs, a fashionably ripped T-shirt that skimmed my tits and hung straight down off them, and the high-heeled mules we all wore. That night and every night, and every afternoon, and some mornings, he had me walk the length of the warehouse while he straddled a chair and stroked his cock, all the while talking softly, almost crooning.

"That's it. And back. Now pull your shirt up. Let me see those titties. Now ... I want you to ... undo your cut-offs. C'mon. Are you wearing panties? Ooooh. Red ones. Good, baby. Well, stop right there and lose those cut-offs. Those? No. Keep 'em on ..."

Shortly after I lost my job as a busgirl, Lloyd and I moved to a small apartment in the Italian district of Vancouver. The place, which was over a delicatessen, had high ceilings, peeling paint, and astonishingly low rent. Lloyd hung an army surplus parachute from the living room ceiling and nailed together a couch, a bed, a kitchen table and some benches from scrap wood, topping the couch with orange cushions he found in a back alley. We slept in the front room because Lloyd's St. Bernard, Snooker, had had her puppies in the bedroom. They yapped constantly and their smell came right out into the hall. Nowhere was my own personality in evidence.

One day Nita, a busgirl at Mallard's, came over to the new apartment for a visit. She was staying in the basement of her sister's house in exchange for looking after her sister's brood, and the husband kept coming downstairs and raping her. Sleepless from ineffectual vigilance, she was barely hanging onto her night shift at the restaurant and, even if she had had time to look for a place, there was nowhere she could afford to go.

Anyway, Nita had noticed an agency down the street advertising for "Exotic Dancers."

An employment crunch was on. Waitresses were running around with two-page résumés. I couldn't compete. I was afraid of the well-dressed, conservative adults in authority positions that all employers seemed to be.

The agency, on lower Commercial Drive, was wedged between a joke shop and a store that sold salami. Pro-Media Enterprises Inc. was spelled out in an arch of gold press-on letters; the 'n' in Inc. had slipped into the dead flies gathering dust on the sill. The Venetian blinds that covered both windows were drawn. Cautiously, Nita and I entered. We were soon joined by a third girl, tall, who was trying to raise money for her second year of college. We were wearing leotards like the ad said, so we stripped down to them in the large, dusty room, and stood around looking at the promo shots on the walls.

Glamorous faces with black-rimmed eyes and drawn-on beauty marks smiled down at us or pouted seductively. "XOXOXO, Morganna," was scrawled across a photo of a heavily-made-up blonde with the biggest breasts I'd ever seen, straining against the fabric of a wet T-shirt. "Baseball's Kissing Bandit," the typed caption read. Sure enough, she wore a ballcap. In another photo two women, a blonde and a brunette, stood back to back, each leaning forward in her high-heeled shoes. They wore baby doll nighties. Each held a teddy bear. In another, a woman stood in what looked like a giant clamshell. A snake wound between her legs, around her breasts, and up against her long white throat. Looking closer, I saw she was wearing a fig-leaf G-string.

"Ladies. You are here to see me, yes?" We turned to see a plump man in a mauve silk shirt busily looking us up and down. Clyde DuBois. He stood near a doorway from which came the faint clicking whir of sewing machines. The next thing I remember we were all self-consciously sashaying around the room to the crackling recording of a bump-and-grind horn solo, administered by Clyde, via the ancient console record player.

"One, two, three, UP. Zat's it. No, no, no. Not like zat—like *zis*. You must *rrroll* ze hips!" So saying, he would tilt his chin skyward and strut, hurling his ample, baggy-trousered bottom from side to side. At one point he opened a desk drawer and withdrew a feather boa before continuing, this time augmenting his strut with far-flung gestures of astonishing languor and grace. He was short, hot-tempered, and full of *joie de vivre*. We tried not to giggle.

At the same time, he seemed to know what he was talk-ing about and we wanted to impress him. At least I did. For in the end, only I went back for lessons, the third girl hav-ing dropped out ("I don't think it's my thing"), and Nita having been kindly persuaded that her talents lay elsewhere.

Did I have talent then? I suppose so. Gliding through the dusty studio in the late afternoon, my hips slid easily from side to side, caressed by the velvety trumpet. Clyde eyed me narrowly, crooning, by turns encouragingly— "Oui. C'est belle. A natural"—and threateningly— "Slower ... slo-wer. *Regarde. Comme ça.*" After perhaps a week of this, he led me through to the back, where his costumiers, three middle-aged women who seemed to live at their sewing machines, gathered around me with measuring tapes, communicating in odd grunts and hisses since each had a mouthful of pins.

After much poking and patting and clucking on the part of the women, Clyde fronted me two costumes: a deep blue spangled G-string with frilled T-bar and padded bra, headpiece and filmy cape—a "chiffon"—to wear over top, and an evening gown of black and gold brocade. The gown unzipped from the floor, slowly revealing ankle, calf, thigh, right up to my armpit, where it came daintily undone and could be flung aside using the classic lasso motion Clyde had taught me. It came with a full set of matching brocade underpieces and elbow gloves. I signed a form saying I had purchased the costumes and would "work them off."

I took the bus downtown and bought black spike heels at Army and Navy, and stockings and a wide black garter belt that covered all but the top inch of my scar at Orpheum Lingerie. One of the window mannequins wore a diaphanous, cupless mauve peignoir with tiny, glittery, gold-and-mauve G-string and gauntlettes, and the other, a red basque with black lace-trimmed garters and matching red-seamed stockings. Inside, you could buy marabou-trimmed mules to match, as well as feather boas, crotch-less panties, G-strings, elbow gloves, fingerless elbow gloves (gauntlets) or wrist gloves (gauntlettes), seamed stockings, and baby dolls, in every shade and pattern from leopard print to after-midnight black to metallic snake-skin bronze.

Maude and Lucille, the two white-haired sisters who ran the store, looked me up and down and beamed.

"Are you one of Meg's girls? We give ten percent off to dancers."

"I'm with Pro-Media."

"Ah. Clyde. That's just fine. Fine."

Lucille, in cardigan and cameo pin, folded my purchases in tissue paper.

"We've a special on crotchless undies," Maude informed me brightly, accepting my last ten-dollar bill.

Noon, Tuesday, August 9
12 Commercial Drive
Just woke up.

I leave for my first stripping gig next week. My contract is with The Duncan Inn, which is a Greyhound and then a ferry ride to Vancouver Island. They'll provide my room, but not food or transportation. Six shows a day, Monday through Saturday. The owner will pay me after my last show, and will send Clyde's percentage to him. All contracts in this business are "No play, No pay," Clyde explained: payment only on completion of *all* your shows, or leave empty-handed.

"That's it? Just my signature?" I'd signed Tabitha.

"Your signature is all that's needed." Clyde folded his arms and smiled.

"No ID? Don't you even want my real name for your files?"

Clyde looked down for a moment, then straight into my eyes. "Nobody needs to know your real name."

I'm lucky to have Lloyd for a boyfriend. I owe him so much—he's been supporting me since I got fired from Mallard's. He cooks for me and tries to teach me about internal combustion engines, how to roll a tight joint, and how to deep throat. ("Things you'll need to know in life," he says.) He reads a lot about World War II—knows dates, names, places. But mostly, he teaches me about music. He plays songs off records, one after another, and you're supposed to just sit there and try not to read because he wants to look in your eyes (tapping his cowboy boots, "conducting" with his fingers, while his crazy eye wanders the walls), point out who the producer was and who's playing backup steel guitar and how the lyrics foretell the singer's eventual death by OD or plane crash or choking on a sandwich.

I'm nervous about the upcoming bookings. I still want a normal job, but all the ads say experience and I don't have any.

Sometimes when Lloyd's not home I sit in the closet like this and write in the coil notebook I keep hidden in a milk crate with my clothes. Apart from my toothbrush in the bathroom, and a duffle bag of things I've started to put together for dancing, they're the only visible signs of my existence. Soon they'll have to be moved to the puppy room, Lloyd tells me; he wants to try growing dope in here under mixed-spectrum fluorescents.

2 a.m. Monday, August 15
The Duncan Inn, Duncan

This pen is now being held by a stripper. Just got offstage from my first show—sweating. Twenty minutes of striptease is *work!* Can't believe I'm going to do six shows a day, six days straight.

Now I know what it feels like to fall from an airplane. Or, every now and then you hear about some farm kid who loses a hand in a hay baler. He wraps it up in his blood-soaked shirt and flags a passing truck and, several days later in the newspaper, is shown grinning and holding out his arm, a circlet of barbed wire stitches around the wrist. You never know what you're going to do until you're doing it.

I really want to be good at something.

(Tearful conversation with Lloyd from the lobby phone.

"I've changed my mind. I'm coming home."

"The hell you are. You're broke, if you'll recall. You don't have money for the bus back, and I'm sure as hell not bailing you out. Just do your six shows a day like a good girl, and you'll get paid on Saturday night. You signed Clyde's contract, remember? And I put a lot of work into those tapes. So why don't you just go for a walk and smoke a joint.")

The stage is about eight-by-six feet. I was just starting to shimmy around it, wishing I'd thought to practise with my new shoes in shag, when eight big guys in stubble and black leather and boots and studs and chains clanked in and put their boots up on the wrought-iron railing that runs in front.

I felt like the hostess at a party where it really matters that the hors-d'oeuvres are delicious and that there are enough to go around.

Every now and then one of them would spit onto the floor (which is covered in pencil shavings for some strange reason, like a giant hamster cage). Kneeling, I undressed with my back to them, but left my garter belt on. I made eye contact with them in the mirror, and let my hair down slowly, the way I practised in my room last night for hours. It feels surprisingly natural, undressing for a lot of men. Intimate—just me, in black-and-gold elbow gloves, teasing off my stockings, looking as if nothing had ever happened to mar me, and them, not spitting anymore and hardly moving. Something changed, towards the end, and I saw that I have, if not power, then something they travelled here to see. Something they want.

My father's books lined all the walls of the house, even the kitchen and bathroom. I remember crayoning in empty exam booklets while he marked his students' essays.

"We have Shakespeare like other people have mice," my mother once said.

They made a big deal about Hamlet at school. To me he seemed confused and self-centred; he got a lot of air time. Ophelia, I noticed, got very little; hardly anyone spoke to her, except to tell her to piss off to a nunnery. The teacher and the producers of the film we saw seemed to agree with my father: all that was important about Ophelia was that she was pretty and graceful and had long hair.

What, I wondered, if she'd been a klutz with a mouthful of crooked teeth, like Big Ethel in *Archie* comics? Maybe she would've been free to have some fun at least, to hang out in the stables and smoke with the grooms. But then what? She probably would have killed herself anyway, but without all the ceremony—say, in a trough of dirty water. Off-stage, beyond the margins, and been written out of the text completely.

Dream: I am walking home from school. I have an aerial view of myself, in sweater and skirt, under the maples. My self-conscious stumbling lope, my books held close to my chest. The leaves are down. They make a scuffly sound, like paper bags under my loafers. The bare limbs claw the sky, rake at it as if to draw blood, or to gesture to each other in some malignant language.

Gradually, my figure disappears. The scene remains, only I have been erased.

Sunday, August 21
12 Commercial Drive

Home after my first six days on the road. I got the money!

However. Lloyd reminded me last night he's still supporting me, just by letting me keep some of it to invest in more costumes.

A couple of nights ago, he was sitting in the kitchen with Tod and Fred, his buddies who are my age. I went to fry myself an egg. He came up behind me, peered into the pan and kept up a running commentary: the pan's too hot, the flame's too high, that's my pan anyway, you're not tilt-ing it right, the edge of the white shouldn't be lacy when the yolk's still raw.

"Don't forget, I'm a chef."

"Aren't you just a sous-chef?" I said. That was a mistake. He rocked back on his heels, spatula poised over the pan, and looked me up and down.

"Well, well, Miss High-and-Mighty. And aren't you just an unemployed high school drop-out with zero mar-ketable skills? Oh, no. I forgot. You're a *danceuse,* now." He went up on his toes. Fred snickered; Tod just kept rolling a joint from the heap on the table. He flicked a glance at me, but I couldn't read it. Lloyd was rising above it, sigh-ing, "Never mind. Just wash the dishes and let's not have any more of your high-falutin' bullshit." So now only *he* cooks, and I take up my station facing the wall, and day-dream while nosing the copper wire scrubby into the crusted-over muffin tins.

1:30 a.m. Wednesday, November 9
Dell Hotel, Room 107
King George Highway, Surrey
(This will just be a four-day gig since
they're having a band this weekend.)

"Bend over, baby!"

"Hey, bitch! Show us your hole!"

"Hey, *dar*lin'! Need some help skinnin' that beaver?!" Everybody gets hassled. ("Let's see some pink!" they yell, and we stick out our tongues. They usually laugh, then.) But Shayla—Vixxen—gets it worse than me. Her smile doesn't quite cover her fear, but I'm not sure if that's cause or effect.

I was standing at the bar and she was getting down to a love song, still wearing her majorette's cap, white gloves, white boots. On her back on her rug, a rosebud-sprigged comforter ("My grandmother made it for me when I was eight. I can't sleep without it"), in the radiating waves of her knee-length, wavy hair. Pink lights swirling around the stage. She was teasing off her silver sequinned G, pretending to use the elastic to raise and lower her hips. (Her head thrown back toward the mirror. She could see her breasts beyond the reflection of her upside-down face. Gazing into her own eyes while opening her legs to the men.) It was all going down as smooth and syrupy as a drink served with a tiny paper umbrella when a voice cut through the murmurs of the other men. Like lye, it seemed to me. Because suddenly I was aware of our skeletons, Shayla's and mine.

I'm not going to record what he said. Only that it was harsh, and cruder than either of us are used to. Most of the men moved away from the guy, who was straddling a chair ten feet from centre stage, and swishing his drink around in his mouth like he was thinking of spraying it on her pussy; a few cast curious or apologetic glances at me (I guess since Shayla's face was hidden), but nobody moved. Nobody told him off, never mind threw him out. A few even chuckled. She didn't flinch, but I felt his words go through her, like a breeze across a pond, and I knew she'd left the room, or was up on the ceiling, looking down at us, that all we had of her was her body.

Shayla's asleep across from me now, under a picture of a peasant woman digging potatoes, in this room of drawers that don't open and ugly lamps. One fist clutches a corner of her comforter. The other is curled alongside her mouth.

They phone our room. Some of them are polite, asking for "the, uh, Indian girl. Wondering if she'd like to go to dinner with me. Anywhere she wants." Some just want "the one with big tits. Do you know if she works on the side?"

We were surprised when we met here, Monday morning.

"What are *you* doing here?!"

"Same as you. *Sha*kin' it, bay-beh." We snapped our fingers and sashayed a bit, giggling. "I just started. This is my third week. You?"

"Fourth." We knew each other briefly, in the winter of tenth grade, before she dropped out. I had sat on the floor by her bed in the group home, while her half-sister had watched "Bugs Bunny" with some of the other kids downstairs. Shayla had picked at her nail polish and showed me the bead earrings she'd made on the reserve.

"My granny taught me. I loved my granny, but she died."

"You're so pretty," I said. She bit her lip, not looking up. "You're prettier than Fawn and Deirdre and the rest of those stuck-up girls at school. That's why they were mean to you—they're jealous."

She looked up, scornful. "They've never seen me without makeup, though. I hate my face without it."

Thursday, November 10

"You know what I'd like?" Shayla has calmed down to where her eyes, blazing above her tight, hard smile when she got off-stage after her last show, have banked down to a bitter glow. It's 2 a.m. and we're finally done showering and removing our makeup. We're lying on our sides on the twin beds, rubbing cream into our feet and looking at tall blond models in magazines. Hers are standing around on a sailboat, gazing out to open sea. Mine are lounging in lace on white, wrought-iron furniture. "I'd like to do something to those men—those pigs. One of them actually spat on me as I was leaving the room. I turned around to see who'd done it but they were all watching the game. Hah!"

"What do you want to do?"

"Give 'em shocks when they misbehave. Every time one of 'em leans forward and sticks his tongue out and wiggles it and raises his eyebrows, it'll be like, 'EEE-OWCH! Wha-wha-whatwazzat?!'"

"It'll be like, 'Don't even think about throwing that ice cube, pal.'"

"No, I know." She sits up. "I've got it." Draws her comforter around her so she is hooded in a nest lined with that thick, copper-lit hair. "Let's us be dressed, and we'll make them take off their clothes."

"Yeah. One at a time. Lock the door so nobody leaves. 'Hey you in the Budweiser ball cap. Yeah, you with the beer gut. Get over on that stage and take it all off so we can get a good look atcha.'"

"We'll sit back and pick our teeth and say, 'She-it. Call yourself a man? Your poor wife must live in fear of suffocating.'"

"Next. Yeah, you, droopy-face. Smile. That's more like it. Now turn around. How sad. Flabby butt and—make a muscle, would ya? Oh, you are making a muscle?"

"Better shape up or you'll never work again."

"Next. Hey, you're kind of cute. Lie down, spread your legs, and raise your ass so—"

"—we can get a good look at your balls." She draws a moustache on her bikini'd sailorette with eyeliner pencil.

"Hey, look at this." I show her six pages of naked faces, one per page, in a section titled "Fix Your Flaws." There isn't a damn thing wrong with any of their faces. It's like they were born airbrushed. She bounces over and settles in beside me. We dump our makeup bags out on the bedspread, with its green and purple amoebas-eating-inkblots pattern, and spend the next little while carefully afflicting

32

the models with moles, warts, Frankenstein scars, and thought bubbles that say, "I'm stupid. Wanna dance?" Or simply, "Shit for brains." She works the left page; I work the right. We give them kohl-black teeth with gold fillings. I use an earring to poke holes through my model's cheeks from the other side of the page. "Bad acne," I explain. "Pass the two-tone blusher."

As she finishes giving the last girl mouldy green earlobes with her "Seafoam-and-Moss" EyeDuo, Shayla lays down the sponge-tip applicator, turns to me, and says, "I know. Let's have a bubble bath."

"I'd like to," I say, yawning, "but I'm falling asleep." I can't risk her seeing my scar.

"Me, too." She sighs, and I squeeze her arm, and it's over, the two of us lying on our backs in our own beds, awake but not talking. Somebody breaks a bottle out in the parking lot. Yelling, car doors slamming, all against the steady whisper of traffic on the King George Highway. I would've washed her shoulders, and between her fingers and toes. Gently.

6 a.m. Friday, November 11
(Remembrance Day)

Shayla's still asleep. She's moving over to the North Burnaby Inn today, an hour's bus ride towards Vancouver. Then she'll do the Ocean Beach in White Rock, starting

Monday morning. I'll go home until Sunday, when I'll take a fifteen-hour bus ride to Prince George in time for Monday morning check-in.

Yesterday, while she was doing her pyjama set for the 12:15 (salesmen from the used car lot across the street doing obscene things to their martini olives while she winked at them and dragged her half-sister's old teddy bear around the stage), I bought two yards of pink velvet ribbon from the Fabricland in the mini-mall next door, where posters advertised patterns for pyjamas, teddy bears, and angel dolls. In one, a little blond girl in a velveteen jumper swung on a stuffed satin moon ("For Your Own Precious Angel").

Last night when we were all packed and showered and nightied, I combed her hair and braided the ribbon in, then we got into our beds and fell asleep in the dark that was tinted with pink neon from the EXXOTIC ACTS sign above our names on the marquee, THIS WEEK FEATURING VIXXEN AND TABITHA. Woke to the sound of truckers pulling in for flapjacks. Thought she was asleep but she whispered,

"Sarah?"

"Yeah?"

"When you were little, were you ever, you know, touched?"

"Sort of."

"Sort of?"

"My bum. Doctors."

"Same thing."

"Think so?"

"Sure."

"Why?"

"Just wondered."

"You?"

"My uncles. On the reserve. They weren't really my uncles." In the long silence that followed, a door opened down the hall, a man clumped past, and an eighteen-wheel rig started up below, blasting shreds of steel guitar and a man singing about a "two-tamming woe-man." I thought she'd fallen back asleep when she whispered,

"I did something terrible. Worst thing I ever did."

"What was that?"

"Leroy and I were at home in the trailer park. I asked him why he didn't have another job yet after the gas station laid him off? I mean, I'm dancing to buy him halide lamps—do you know what those are?" I nod. Lloyd has begun to mention them lately. "He says he'll be able to pay me back with the first pot crop, then I can retire. 'Live like a queen,' he always says. But when I suggested he get another job in the meantime, he got mad and broke my little pony figurine." I'm not supposed to know she's crying.

"So what did you do?"

"I ran out to the shed, thinking I'd hide in there until I felt better, but when I opened the door this little black lab started jumping up and barking and growling at me. I don't know how it got in there. It looked like a demon from hell." She sighs. "No, it didn't. It was almost still a puppy." Long pause. "I kicked it and kicked it, deeper and deeper into the shed. It pissed itself and I didn't stop. Lucky for it there was a loose board in the back wall, behind the lawnmower, and it got away. It hadn't done anything. I'm going to hell."

I fumble around in the night-table drawer and toss Shayla a tissue. "If you're going to hell, we can hang out together."

Saturday, November 12
12 Commercial Drive
Back home for the weekend.

Mallard's has shut down. Between Tod and Fred and Lloyd's Mexican friends from the restaurant, our apartment is like a drop-in centre for unemployed guys.

("I got some Eldorado Red, man. Eet's preem-yum.")

They talk sports, cars, recent crimes, ancient torture methods, how you could commit the ultimate robbery. Most days the nailed-together kitchen table is hidden in smoke, beer bottles, dirty plates, *R. Crumb* comics, drug scissors, papers, and roaches. I walk around, or sit on the fire escape and wonder where I'm supposed to be, if this were real life.

The town stinks of what I thought was boiled cabbage but turns out to be the pulp mill. I dragged in finally at 6 a.m. It's a long, loose shift here—six shows each spread out between noon and eight, with swimsuited house dancers in between. Go-go girls don't cost management nearly as much as we do, and they give the guys something to ogle between shows, so they'll hang around and drink.

I met Alexandra for the first time when I knocked on her door just now.

"Come on in. I'm stretching."

"Oh. But I have the noon show, right? So you're not on till tonight."

"I know," she said airily, looking over my shoulder, "but I have a strict routine. I used to be in the ballet."

I turned to follow her eyes, but all I saw through the grimy window was a Safeway, sulphurously lit against the grey day. Small figures like board-game pieces sleepwalked in and out of the electric door. "The ballet? You're kidding! Which one?"

"Oh, The Royal Winnipeg."

"This place is some dive, isn't it?" I sat on the bed since there was no chair, feeling ugly and inelegant, as I always do around pretty women, or even women who just think they are.

"Oh, I've seen worse," she said. She laughed her tinkly laugh, spritzing something on her face from a cut-glass atomizer.

"What is that stuff?"

"This? Oh, Evian." She gave the word a Parisian spin.

"I've never seen anyone do that outside of *Vogue*."

She looked startled for a moment, then turned a pitying look on me. "My dear, it's *essential* to a good complexion. Of course, I have sensitive skin. All my cosmetics are hypo-allergenic. I *never* lend eye makeup—or borrow it, for that matter. Once I made that mistake in a group dressing room. I was just about to lift the wand to my face when I saw something move. Can you imagine? I looked closer and there were all these tiny white things ... crawling. Ugh," she shuddered. "Disgusting."

"What about earrings?" I said. Do you have to be careful about—?"

"—Gold. I can only wear pure gold. Eighteen carat or higher. I mostly just wear my diamonds."

She was doing *pliés* in her black lace leotard, having paused to rub vaseline on her hands and slip them into white cotton gloves. Again, her eyes were not on me but past me. I had the sense that I was intruding on something intimate, then saw that I was between her and her mirror image and moved back.

"What about surgical steel?"

"Excuse me?"

"In your ears."

"Oh. Oh no. Much too crude. Why, once I bought a pair of rather *expensive* amethyst drops from Saks Fifth Avenue in New York. Do you know, they turned my earlobes green? Green! Can you imagine?"

7:40 p.m. Monday
(Alexandra doing the can-can on-stage.)
Playgirl Cabaret, scribbling between shows.

We change in a translucent cubicle in the middle of the bar. Since the cubicle is lit and the bar is dark, our silhouettes are thrown like one big, girlie shadow-lantern. Yes, folks, you can watch us as we thrash in and out of tight skirts, do up each other's zippers, and bend over in our high heels to reach for a bra from our respective heaps of stockings, gloves, T-bars, G-strings, boas, dusters, etc.

"Do you book through Clyde, too?"

"No, I book through Meg. She's got the most out-of-town gigs."

"What's she like?"

"Oh, Meg's grand. She's the oldest of ten kids from West Virginia. 'Broke my momma's heart,' she always says, 'when I ran away from home at fourteen and took up striptease.' She's six feet tall and has straight brown hair to her waist. If a girl gets sick and she can't get a replacement, she'll show up and say, 'Hi—I'm Lulubelle from Fort McMurray,' and do the shows herself."

"We ought to be charging for this. Does this bra look okay?"

"Well, here. Pin these shoulder pads in before you put it on, or they'll know what you're doing. Makes your breasts look bigger. Didn't anyone ever show you this?"

"Uh-uh. Sort of like those sandwiches you get with the meat all bunched up in the middle? You nibble out to the crust and there's just mayonnaise and a few shreds of lettuce." She gives me a weird look. "Never mind."

"You're lucky. I had to leave the ballet because of these. Of course, they got me into *Playboy*—"

"You were in *Playboy*?"

"Bunny of the Year."

"You're kidding! What year?"

"Oh now, I forget. But I have it around somewhere. I'll show you later. Oops! I'm on."

The men like her better than me. Her costumes are glitzier; she has TV-lady flash. Dances to Edith Piaf. The audience, mostly grizzled ex-prospectors, millworkers and laid-off same, actually sings along. Whether their eyes are suspicious, hostile, bleary or bored, something about A. reaches them and by the end of the first number they are raising their beer glasses and warbling "Chanson d'Amour" along with Edith. This phenomenon must be seen to be believed.

Fingering the flocked silhouette of the ideal naked woman on a matchbook, I look slowly around the bar, watch the bikers glance at Alexandra and look away, glance back when she drops her G and stay looking while she does her floor—mainly the old gynecology-exam position, legs scissoring for added interest and yes, toes pointed—and think, I am somebody pretending to be somebody pretending to be somebody else.

They like my Motorcycle Mama set, which consists of torn, very short cut-offs, hot pink T-shirt ripped cave-woman style, leather jacket and spikes. Fast, easy, cheap. The costume, that is. (They also go for my Bayou Stomp set. A. and I are about as different as you can get and still fit the job description.) Wayne, a.k.a. Animal, seems to be the leader. He and his sidekick, Tiny (six feet five), are crazy about my rose perfume.

Management likes to see you socializing in the bar when you're not on-stage. So I've spent the last several between-shows at their table, streaming sweat, gulping grapefruit juice and listening to Tiny's explanation of what can go wrong with a Harley's exhaust.

"It's all a matter of timing. If the pistons misfire ..." Does he think I even know what a piston looks like? Still, he carries on earnestly, words like "valve" and "com-bustible" occasionally surfacing over a tide of Edith Piaf. But it's Wayne's rare glance that connects. He walks with a limp, leaning on a stick, and has grey streaks in his long brown hair.

"What I like about being a biker," Wayne tells me, "is we're the dregs, the bottom, the lowest of the low. There's nowhere to fall."

I look into mirrors every chance I get. I keep hoping I will catch myself looking like the sort of woman nations go to war over—feminine, delicate, romantic. Instead my reflection has no taste and no colour, like water. But I keep trying, the way when you lose something you look over and over in the same places.

Chuck, the manager, who according to Wayne is up for six counts of child molesting, took A. aside after her noon show today and told her to "quit playing that frog music." She was peeved but, to give her credit, has rallied gamely by descending on the music shop next to the Safeway and buying an armload of sound tracks to musicals. It's a dark afternoon. I've been asleep most of the day. Now I'm painting my toenails with "Rubyfruit," alone in this big room (although Alexandra's is bigger and has a tub—she got here first), but assailed from all sides: "Hello Dolly" has slid in under the door while the smell of sizzling bacon rises through the heat vent from the restaurant below. "Hello Dolly?" I roll my eyes like Father Mulcahey on "M.A.S.H." Saints preserve us.

A. says she's twenty-eight, and that she's never lived with a man. Okay, I believe her.

"I'm the rebellious one in my family," or "I live from day to day," she'll pronounce, with a little flush of self-pleasure.

The men in town know Room 220 and 221 are the dancers' rooms. Any time, you can look down and see at least one guy standing in the parking lot, looking back up at you.

"Wayne, can you help me? I can't find my pink lace G-string."

"What do you think, boys? Can we help her?" I was waiting to do my 7:15, sitting at their table in my secretly horny schoolteacher get-up, my hair in a bun held with an HB pencil. "No problem," he told me.

Later, in my room, taking off the crotchless pantyhose that I leave on throughout, he knocked on my door. He whipped the G from the pocket of his plaid flannel shirt, and presented it to me with a flourish and a little bow, his big, rough-knuckled hand on his cane, trembling a little.

"How——?"

"Little friendly persuasion. Tiny lined 'em all up and, very slowly, said,

'Which of you stole my old lady's panties?' Nobody moved for a while. Finally one of the young guys from the mill reached into his shirt and handed it over."

He took me out for dinner. A woman with long blond hair played the harp, sprinkling notes down on us. We kept an eye on the Harley.

"Eat your steak," Wayne said. "Drink your milk."

43

Later, I ran a tub for him, sat with him while he had his bath. Shampooed his head. ("Mmm. That's nice. That's real nice. I like the way you scritch little circles with your nails.") Afterwards, when I had mine, I jumped when he walked in.

"You forget," he said. "I've seen you naked."

"Oh yeah. Right. I forgot." But this is the first time you've seen my front, I thought. Carefully, he lowered himself to the edge of the tub and then slowly, silently traced my scar from my pubic hair up to my fourth rib. I sat up, then, and we kissed, soft and brief.

11 p.m. Wednesday

I decided to try Alexandra with something less personal—say, politics. After all, she said she spent two years in Israel. Turns out politics bore her. She enjoyed her stay in Israel, though. Her brother was there—now he's in Zambia—in his capacity as a mercenary soldier. I get the feeling she doesn't understand me when I talk but that's probably just because she isn't listening. And yet there is a kind heart, somewhere, in there. (I picture a gift shop heart-shaped box nestled in layers of tissue.) She did, for instance, offer to French braid my hair. She did a nice job, too. ("I used to do chignons and braids for all the women in the ballet.")

Tonight went okay. I seem to have caught up in audience

response. I even got an encore. Every floorshow I've been aware of big Patti, the assistant bar manager, watching me intensely from behind the bar. I glanced towards her once but only saw my naked pink body reflected in her thick glasses. She acts like she hates me.

I can hardly wait to scrub the thin scum of Prince George off my skin.

After I got off-stage for the noon show, Kelly and Kim, the go-go girls, were in the changing box, ironing, of all things.

"It's for that bitch Patti. She lives with Chuck—oh, didn't you know? They make the two of us do their work."

"Look at this," said Kim. "Could you guess by looking at him he likes his underwear ironed?"

"They have kids?" I was looking at a separate, smaller heap of tiny dresses and rumpled sheets with teddy bears printed on them.

"No," said Kelly. "Since Wednesday's ironing day, I always bring in my daughter's stuff. Saves me doing it Sundays. I hardly get to see her as it is, since she's at day-care during the days and I work at night. The stupid thing is, daycare costs almost as much as I make. But I have to work. Welfare makes you feel—I wasn't raised to take handouts."

"I know what you mean," I said.

"At least this job pays pretty good. Except," she grimaced down at the iron, which was busily exploring a shirt with Chuck's monogram on the collar, "if you figure in the extra work. I make good tips, too, and I don't have to take off my clothes. Oops," she added, and suddenly started to fuss with getting the shirt onto a hanger.

"It's okay," I said. "Stripping's not for everybody."

"I know," she said quickly. "You make way more money than I do. To tell the truth, sometimes I think about it. I mean, I couldn't take Jenny on the road but there's two places here in town and I could leave her with my mother. But, really, I know it's not for me. I was raised Methodist and—"

"So was Holy Tara," I said. "Mind you, she does seem to have left the church. Have you seen her crucifix routine?"

Kelly smiled. "Anyway—" She put down the iron.

"You're worried about stretch marks?"

"No. Actually, I had Jenny so young I don't have stretch marks. It's just I never thought of myself like that. Like this." She gestured through the door to the bar, where Chuck could be seen polishing glasses. He paused to look over at her and she hastily picked up the iron again. "If I went in deeper I'd have to lay out money for more costumes, my own promo, transportation, tapes. As it is, I only have to have three costumes, cab fare one way since I walk to work, and Chuck provides the music. He even did our promo."

"Of course," put in Kim, ironing a Patti-sized blouse, "he wanted it done his way."

In the glassed-over case outside are the promo photos of Kelly and Kim, in identical mini sailor suits and sailor hats, flanking Alexandra in her G-string and headdress, and me, carefully twisted with a feather boa at my waist, smiling with a snarl, whippet lean. Kelly and Kim bend in toward us, like B-girls in a newsreel. Like they are leaning over to wave goodbye to sailors on an aircraft carrier, gazing brightly into the future strong and free. If you know Kelly you can make out a look of distraction, as if her mind is concentrating on someone beyond the lens. But only if you look.

"Like I was saying," said Kelly, when Kim went to put more water in the iron, "this way it's more casual. Almost like a secretarial job. Actually," she gives her soft, low half-laugh, "the first couple of years I was here I was exclusively on mornings—No," she adds, seeing my puzzled look, "Chuck did away with it. Wasn't making a profit, he said. I told my mother I was a secretary. She doesn't get out much so she bought it. But when he changed our hours I had to tell her. I think she would've cut me out if it weren't for Jenny. Anyway, this job is okay for now. But I'm not," she nods toward Kim, "like her. This is only temporary."

Lunch earlier with Alexandra and Tiny at The Wagon Wheel Café. Tiny insisted on buttering my roll. He stole ketchup for me from the next table, his gangly descending arm reminding me of the sideshow game where you put a quarter in the box and the mechanical arm goes after a prize. I believe he would've cut my meat. Alexandra was holding forth about her brilliant career.

"What's this?" said Tiny, escorting something out of the sugar bowl. "Looky here. An ant."

"You want to talk about *ants*," said A. "Why, when I was in the Amazon ..."

I threw Tiny a martyred glance.

"Been reading this novel about a monster who eats bike parts," he said, his spidery fingers closing rhythmically on three French fries and folding them into his mouth. "There are different species of monsters but they're all the same general type."

"Like dinosaurs," I put in.

"Exactly. But they're hybrids. Mechanobiological. The author explains it real well. The Bugatrons eat Italian bikes, the Kawatrons eat the Jap crap, and—"

"Who eats the Harleys?"

He held up a hand. "Please. I'm getting to that. The Armaggetrons eat the Harleys. You see, people as we know them have passed from the earth. Too weak—their parts kept breaking down. Only a super-race of mechanics remain. Their training is a mix of medical surgeon and bike mechanic—you know, 'Physician, heal thyself?'

Anyway, they're under oath to care for all the bikes but they sort of favour the Harleys. Of course," he shrugs modestly, almost poking me in the eye with a ketchupped fry, "Harleys are what they ride themselves. This puts them at the greatest risk of being attacked by an Armaggetron, which are the biggest, most aggressive monsters—well, them and the Kawatrons, who have one big eye and a lot of horns."

"I read, too," said Alexandra. "I'm partial to the romances of Violet Suzanna Vale."

"Uh-huh," Tiny and I said at the exact same time, our carefully neutral tone identical.

"They're very well written. They're set in England or Scotland at the turn of the century. I was a Rebel clanswoman, you know, in a past life. Once I went to a psychic? She said—"

"What about the books?" said Tiny, displaying what struck me as uncharacteristic interest in romance novels. He had produced a pocket-sized motorbike from somewhere and was running it up and down the napkin dispenser.

"They always have a heroine," said Alexandra, blotting her lips in highly ladylike fashion. Something more complicated came over her face, something quiet. She fiddled with the paper tube her milkshake straw had come in, twisting it and untwisting it, then twisting it the other way.

"What else?" I asked. Tiny was sitting back, his long arm out, curving around his plate. He held the bike along the rim. Briefly, he flicked his eyes up at her but she didn't notice.

"Nothing. Just … she always gets married at the end."

When I'm on the circuit, I often like to go to the library disguised as a respectable woman in a dress and flat shoes. Sometimes, especially in the tiniest towns, a man will do a double take, but rarely. Simple creatures, they don't seem to recognize a woman from one clothing change to the next. But I can understand: when I'm eating a BLT, I don't want to think about pesticides on the vegetables or carcinogens in the bacon.

I also like to browse in bookstores. Not that I can read a book when I'm on the road. I think it's asking just a little too much of myself to go from impersonating (pick one): a nymphomaniacal underpaid service worker (French Maid) or oversexed zoo animal or gymnastically inclined schoolteacher or enthusiastic bride to, say, *Tess of the D'Urbervilles* (whose problems, come to think of it, are depressingly similar to mine).

8 a.m. Saturday, November 19
Satan's Angels' Lodge
Just outside Prince George.

The den: fake wood panelling, black velvet painting of

curvaceous brown-eyed woman on a Harley, plaid horse-hair sofa and chairs. Wayne gazed into his Jack Daniels, moved it in a circle and the amber slopped, clinging to the glass.

"You remind me a bit of my second. Misty. Yeah, she was my shadowmate. Skinny like you. Sweet, too. Like you."

Last night we had moose meat the boys grilled outside. ("This little one hugs me up nice and tight," he told the others as they barbecued our dinner.)

"Pour me another one," he said.

"You sure? You won't get drunk and attack me? I would-n't like that, you know."

"I won't. I promise."

"Here," I said. "So what happened?"

"She died in a crash. We were swinging low over Johnson's Pass—she had her own bike—and she was hit by a Camaro." Later, in bed, my bare thighs silky and vulner-able against him. He swallowed whiskey, "for the pain."

Wayne limps because he's going to die. He's got a degenerative bone disease, something to do with the disks in his spine.

"It's a wheelchair if they operate," he said. "No way. When the time comes, I'm gonna get on my Harley and ride. I've got the cliff picked out. My boys will be around me; we'll have a ceremony, then they'll watch me go. I'm gonna die like a man."

The boys kept putting their heads around the door. "Hey, hey, hey. Animal's got it made, man."

"Any room for me in there?"

"Beat it," he told them. "She needs her sleep." He could've raped me. We both knew it. I wouldn't have tried to press charges. Just a biker rolling a peeler, they'd say. She asked for it.

("Anything you say," he murmured into my hair. "But darlin'? Do like you did earlier—cuddle up close.") In the morning I found a knife under the pillow. He tucked it in his jacket, inside. I froze, just for a second.

"Come here a minute." I followed him down the hall, into a bedroom with blacklight posters. He opened a drawer containing a gun and some badges. "I was the president." He glanced at me. Shyly?

"Neat," I said.

Sunday morning, November 20
Wayne's, Prince George

Paid! I survived another thirty-six shows! God, it felt good last night after my last show when Chuck counted out my stack of hundred-dollar bills and I shoved them in my boot. I rode away with Wayne—liking his solidity, the scent of his leather, the comforting purr of the bike between my legs—and slept on his couch last night.

Wayne's going to drive me to the coast ("have to see a man about a girl") since I've got nothing booked for this week.

His ramshackle wood-frame house is near the Playgirl. Bikes all over the yard. His woman, Jan, is a fitness instructor. She's nineteen—a year and a bit older than me—and has dark curly hair and a real beauty mark. Her cheeks flush when she talks about skiing. I sat cross-legged on the lino late last night, leaning against the wall next to the woodstove, and watched her take a bath.

"You love Wayne." I said it as sort of a question.

"Yeah," she said. "Wayne's nice. But, he's kinda old for me. I might leave him in the spring."

Monday, November 21

"Your old man know how lucky he is?"

"Yeah," I say, uncertainly.

"I don't think so or he'd be with you." He's filling up the gastank. It's a crisp, clear day on the Goldrush Trail section of the Yellowhead Trans-Canada Highway, in Soda Creek, coming up on Williams Lake. All around us, black and white cattle graze on rolling golden hills. I can smell sawmill smoke and hear the Fraser River below us.

"Either he doesn't know the job is dangerous—that means he's an idiot—or he doesn't care."

"Buy me a Fudgesickle?"

He laughs. My freckles have come out in the sun. No makeup since I'm off, my hair in pigtails.

"You look about twelve," he says. The Fudgesickle drips

on my fingers and I lick them, then it suddenly falls off the stick and I'm eating it out of my hand, laughing and spluttering and making a mess. I feel his gaze on me, warm like the sun overhead.

"Naomi, my second wife, she died bearing me a son." We were sitting in the Husky station in Cache Creek, having just passed Lone Butte and signs pointing off to Alkali Lake, Dog Creek, and Gang Ranch. "I was working for the Chow family and they took him from me. Said if you want to see your ass alive you'll be over city limits by midnight. They raised my boy. I don't want him now."

"The Chow family?"

He looked at me a moment. "They're a crime family, operate out of Chinatown. I did," he pauses, "bodywork for them. Ran drugs. Smuggled 'em. Sold 'em. Me and my boys still control all the drugs in Prince George, and the hookers, too."

"Protect them, like?"

"Well, sometimes we have to beat a girl up, or get an enforcer. That's when …"

"I don't think I want to know."

"You're right, little mama."

I know what he meant by "bodywork" now. He turned his head away from me on the pillow when he told me he stabbed a man in the kidney with an ice pick. I rubbed his neck and he closed his eyes. Without lipstick, without sequins, without perfume, without lace, I knelt over him in my white cotton undies and cradled his neck on my forearms, rolling it back and forth to relax the muscles. Nearby, his jacket hung over a chair.

His face is pouchy with deep wrinkles. He smells like baby powder.

We were sitting up in bed in The Beaver Dell Motel, eating cold, deep-fried wontons out of a little white carton when I saw the grainy footage on the 6 o'clock news: a theatrical agency had burned. Bales of sparkly fabric were piled on the fire escape. The cameraman's hands shook as he focussed on them; the mike picked up the forlorn ping of drops hitting the wrought iron. Sequinned organza, lamé, yards and yards of tulle, opulent and abandoned like once-beautiful women, shimmered in the rainy dusk.

I heard later that Clyde took what remained of his glittery stock and went to Las Vegas, where he helped start the School of Striptease. And Alexandra was right about Meg—she was a good agent.

"Hiya, Howie. As ever. Wednesday morning and I'm up to my ass in alligators. Everybody's calling in for their bookings. Say, there's a new girl here—a model, she says. Can you hold? Tammy Tease, you're at the Cold Balls—I mean the Cobalt—this week ..."

The agency walls are papered in promo shots, black-and-white and colour, of brunette, blond and redheaded women, black women, Asian women, women on Harleys, women in wet T-shirts holding teddy bears, women licking foam from champagne bottles, women glistening with baby oil, women wearing eight square inches of sequinned fabric, women sipping from low drinking fountains in short shorts, women who pressed their lips, scarlet, magenta, crimson, coral, pink or Weekend-In-Paris red to their photos after signing with lots of luv.

"The *Cobalt*?" Tammy jammed a soother into her baby's mouth. Meg lowered her voice.

"It's just till you get your figure back."

"Last time I did the Cobalt there were used Sheiks all over the stage. Coupla spikes, too. That rathole's junkie heaven."

"You're welcome," said Meg. "I'm pencilling you in. Check-in's at 6 p.m." To the new girl: "It's my ol' bud Howie from the Trapline. Want to go to Fort Nelson?"

Fort Nelson is six hundred and eighty miles north of

Vancouver, just below the border.

"But," said the new girl, biting her lip, "see ... I don't actually really know how to ..."

"D'you dance around your bedroom sometimes?" The new girl nodded. "Get down on your hands and knees. See? Right there, you look attractive to a man." Into the phone, "I got a wild one for you, Howie."

Sunday, December 4
Squamish.

An old man sat up front, talking to the Greyhound driver, who appraised me, straggly and exhausted with my rolled-up rug and ratty luggage, noting the circles under my eyes and said,

"Stripper?" to which I wearily nodded and collapsed into one of the deep seats, where I eavesdropped on the old man's rapturous account.

"She had on this nurse's uniform, see, and boy, did she fill it out. Never seen such tits. Mm, mmm. And legs! The most fantastic legs. Rita Ricardo. Latina, you know? They always have such fine legs. And she went down into the audience, right down among us, and she wiggled her behind and bent over and took out these little pills—they were candy of course—and she pretended to prescribe them. 'Open your mouth,' she'd say, and she'd put one on

57

your tongue. Do you know, she actually put her hand on my forehead? And did I have a fever! Mm, mmm. What a woman. She had more sex appeal in that thick black hair than ten women put together …"

I felt myself rapidly diminishing, watching Burger Kings and used car dealerships go by. Older women try harder. They tell jokes. They use props. They do tricks. Like Mitzi DuPree's ping-pong-balls-ejected-from-vagina routine. "She owns a mink coat and drives a Mercedes," Meg says. "She deserves it. She works hard." I'll bet.

Monday, December 5
Squamish

Called in just now to confirm my Christmas bookings.

What unnerves me about phoning Meg's office is that whether you get her or her sister Tracy or one of the single-mom strippers who hang around, the tone of voice is uniform. Gentle, condolatory, soft, as if they know something and aren't telling. As if they're used to receiving phone calls through tears or a drugged or alcoholic stupor.

("Meg? I'm in Revelstoke. I need help.") How much help would Meg be? I try not to wonder how many times she's been called to the city morgue.

Nearing Kelowna, one of several small, fruit-belt frontier towns. Orchards among brown sagebrush. In the wind howling down from the mountains (salted with white goats), huge wooden signs are whipped back and forth. Portuguese names—Ferreira, DeSanto—accompany gushing cornucopias: apples with little windowpanes in their sides, peaches bleeding internally.

"A lot of girls think, 'I'll fuck him and he'll give me a hundred dollars.' That's just foolish—I can go through a hundred dollars in five minutes." Shalimar says she's twenty-eight, from New York, more recently from L.A. "The sugar-daddy game is where it's at, baby. Think *big*. Get him to pay your rent or at least buy you a car."

I am still lugging around the broken-zippered duffel, still wearing my usual uniform: sweatshirt over T-shirt over tight black jeans, high-top sneakers. Shalimar, in the satin corselet, garter belt and stockings of her "white wedding" set, is fluffing her veil. Her eyes are naturally rimmed in black, and she has enhanced them with kohl. Everything about her is perfect: her long brown legs, delicate shoulders, the haughty tilt of her face, with its fine high cheekbones. She has a way of putting her head back and looking at you almost disdainfully through half-closed eyes.

"Do you think I could?"

I feel her take me in critically. "Why sure," she says after a pause. "Get yourself a fur and some nice-looking clothes and get it *together!*"

"How does it work? Do you go out every night?"

"Oh, no. Nothing like that. I have this one guy. He's seventy-four. I let him fuck me, say, every six weeks. He bought me a Jag. It's back home in L.A. I dated another guy once," she adds. "He bought me a complete set of ski equipment—clothes and all."

Friday, December 23

The atmosphere in the bar two days before Christmas seems to alternate between frantic and depressed. I might as well admit that I'm miserable. It's finally hit me too hard to ignore it—"a day like any other" and all that. The nadir came about an hour ago.

Trish, a.k.a. The Whore of The Willows, sits, pantieless, legs thrown open, at a table with six bikers. Last night I saw her on an old man's lap. Her dress is unbuttoned to the waist, tattoos all over her belly and upper thighs. I was walking through the bar with my tape in hand, rolled-up rug under my arm, after my first show of the day.

"Psst. What have you got on under that thing?" She tries to open my robe. All the men at her table laugh as I pull it closed.

I feel ridiculous. "Later, Trish. Save it."

"Really? Am I invited? I like girls, too." She looked disappointed. Who knows what the world looks like from her eyes? What worries me is I feel like grabbing Trish and a bottle of gold tequila and heading upstairs. We could eat each other out in the shower. (I picture us laughing, shrieking, holding each others' soapy hips in the spray of limitless hotel hot water.) Obliterate these next three days; I wouldn't be the first stripper to rack off fifteen shows drunk. But I know I won't because I'm *saving money*. Pathetic.

Went shopping with Shalimar yesterday morning. You should have seen her strut in her rabbit fur jacket. ("I left my mink in L.A.") She practically spat on the salesgirl at the Bay fragrance counter who couldn't change her thousand dollar bill. It was the first time I'd even seen one. She's invited me to spend Christmas Eve with her and a dancer friend named Lola at the Capri Hotel, "downtown."

"Let's buy party dresses," she said, as I trailed her into Suzy Creamcheese. "It's Christmas. You owe it to yourself." I tried on a shirred lamé cocktail dress and stood there in the dim dressing room regarding myself in the full-length mirror, aware of Shalimar's exquisite feet under the partition. Am I pretty? Sighing, I pulled on my jeans, slid back into the snakeskin cowboy boots that once belonged to Bronwyn, my friend back in high school.

Shalimar modelled a black, fringed twenties number in front of a three-way mirror, lit amber from above. The two salesgirls stood still, gaping at her. With her long neck, high cheekbones, those tapering eyes with built-in black eyeliner, she might have materialized from one of the fashion magazines stashed under the cash register.

"I'm gonna have you wrap it up," she instructed them. "Can you do it up pretty-like, with maybe a gold bow?" They nodded eagerly, wide-eyed. I started to slip away past the racks of sequinned dresses. "Hey. *Hey.* Tabitha. Aren't you gonna buy yourself a dress for the party tomorrow night, girlfriend?" I can feel the salesgirls' cold stares. One was folding a flat, slotted piece of cardboard into a box; the other held scissors and a spool of wrapping ribbon.

Finally I got away, much to Shalimar's annoyance—she seemed to really want me to buy a party dress, but they all cost more than I'd ever spend on a non-costume—and bought myself a lined woollen jacket, very plain, on sale. I'm practical. It's warm.

Later, same day

A guy comes up to me in the bar. Asks, "Do you think you have a warped view of humanity?" As I walk the corridor back to my room, I think, How do I know? How the fuck does anyone know?

"I don't like it," Bronwyn said the last time I talked to her on the phone, when she was home on vacation from law school at Queen's. I saw her sitting out in a courtyard, an open textbook on her lap, surrounded by kneeling, adoring men, like the barbecue scene in *Gone With The Wind*. One of these days she'll graduate. Then what? Prosecute teenaged hookers? "It's not healthy," she said. "It's not ... wholesome." No, I think, spreading tinned paté on a French roll and biting into it. Wholesome it ain't. And yet, compared to my mother's exhausting ideas of what I should be achieving, stripping is oddly restful.

Bronwyn. Long after my father had left, her dad still taught at UBC, specializing in James Joyce. We went to different schools but played together when I was well enough. The summer I was eight I was home on remission, newly infused with someone else's blood. A plumfight in her back garden: we pelted each other with damsons, shrieking and ducking. She threw harder than me ("Don't be such a baby"), but I didn't mind. I was thrilled that she would play with me at all.

Another time she put a Sunlight bottle between her knees and squeezed, crowing, "Look at me! I'm a boy!" then laughed to look up at Ellen and Laura and me, covering our mouths. That was when I think I began my career as wistful spectator. Even now the memory of Bronwyn pedalling up the street in high summer, her hair flying behind her, legs pumping furiously, through a golden haze of catkins (She is waving a stick high in front of her, steering with one hand and yelling. I couldn't ride a bike. I fainted when I ran), sends a rush of saliva to my mouth. I wanted so badly to be her.

I transferred to her high school for our last two years. My mother was working two jobs and was hardly ever at home. Bronwyn often let me sleep at her house, beside her, in that long, high-ceilinged room full of dolls and tin soldiers and fairy books and Beatrix Potter. I woke often to listen to her calm, even breath. My own dreams were full of mushroom clouds exploding over English Bay, Helen Caldicott berating me to dismantle the military industrial complex, and the face of the doomsday clock on the cover of *Time* at one minute to midnight.

Last night I dreamed of Bronwyn on her knees in a cubicle next to me, servicing men with her mouth. It is one of those set-ups like they have in Japan, life-sized women with their legs spread painted on plyboard scrims, our mouths behind the holes where their vaginas would be. The dream is shot in shades of black and grey but her lips are red. Through a tear in the curtain that separates us, I can see a scariform hole in one of her stockings.

The bus pulled into the Vernon depot at 8:20. Deserted, everyone at home drinking eggnog and hugging. The whole town silent except for the young man in a leather jacket and wispy moustache, wanting to smoke me up.

The silence is dripping slowly down around me. Nothing on TV except gospel shit and me without reading material except for the tome on Latin America foisted on me by a fanatic on the bus. Went out walking in my new jacket, which was at least warm, looking for a magazine and a meal. Caught sight of my face in a shop window, white above the black wool. Finally found a Mac's and bought *Seventeen* and a *Penthouse*. Two old women in a station wagon picked me up and we combed the snowy streets looking for an open restaurant. The last place in town was open. So I had Christmas Day dinner in The Pyrogi House with Miss Laura Maclean and her mother, Beth. The goulash was okay.

Here I am in bed with my trusty journal, eating Almond Roca (what the hell), alternately writing and jerking off. (Hey, everyone needs a hobby.) I'd listen to music but my walkman got stolen again. Except for a documentary on the ozone layer, there is nothing on TV but mournful choirs.

At the Capri on Christmas Eve, Shalimar and I met Lola, whose real name was Yolanda MacDonald. She was Cuban-Portuguese and had a serf with her. Actually, he was a businessman from Des Moines, not handsome but not ugly, either. Middling. Lola was tall and sophisto. That afternoon, Shalimar had given me two lines in her room. In that way she's generous, like her insisting I come out with her. But I keep thinking about that poor salesgirl at the Bay fragrance counter that she was so rude to.

Since I hadn't packed for a party, I had on my black leather pants and purple angora sweater. Shalimar and Lola were smug in their fancy, black evening dresses. There was a big box of chocolates open on the luggage stand.

"Help yourself," said Lola. As I chewed a caramel she added, "Take them home, if you like. I don't care for sweets." Lola's Dave poured me champagne and we all did several lines off Lola's alarm clock. Then some Grand Marnier and a couple of coked joints and we set out to go dancing.

Lola and Shalimar linked arms; Dave and I tagged behind, quiet.

"Last Christmas I was in Port-au-Prince," said Lola.

"*I* was in New York at you-know-who's, said Shalimar. "Her apartment is all gold—even the food was gold." We tried a small town honky-tonk called The Zoo. Pool tables, neon beer signs, wooden benches. Deserted but for a clutch of single men posing toughly, alone on Christmas Eve, like us. Lola, Shalimar, and Dave ordered Courvoissier, I ordered tea; we left before long and went to Changes, where a large, deranged dyke asked me to dance. (I declined.) The women ordered Hennessy's with a chaser of black coffee; I ordered white wine and they snickered. Lola rolled another snowcone on the counter of the john while I was peeing. Shalimar ordered fried chicken and had it delivered by cab. When it arrived she ate two bites and was full. I asked the DJ for a song I liked, but he'd never heard of it.

Dave was "intrigued" with my eyes. He wanted to drive me to Vernon. Got back to the Willows at 4 a.m., too coked to sleep, and spent a miserable few hours shaking and staring at my watch.

The bar here in Vernon is tiny. A dive in the classical sense—twenty round tables covered in red terry cloth, jukebox, stage. No poles, no mirrors, no flattering lighting. (I will look like I'm dancing on the lunch counter at Woolworth's. Hell, I already *feel* like a piece of three-day-old lemon meringue pie.) Didn't even notice any pool tables. The staff is nice, though. All middle-aged. Bert, Stan, and Hilda. Both men have made passes at me but Bert, the owner, was kind enough to unlock the kitchen for me at 10:30 last night and fix me fish and chips.

Just got propositioned by a spherical farmer with manure on his rubber boots. ("Not even if I take you to dinner first?" "No. Thank you.") But now, when I'm on my bed, all costumed up and tape rewound just about to go on-stage, and I'm slipping my fingers under my G-string as usual to get in the mood, I can't help hearing Shalimar's words: "They're gonna fuck you anyway. Why not make some money?" My basic fantasy-line is always the same—being fucked from behind by a handful of them, randomly selected from the bar—but now I notice that there has to be money for me to get off.

My painted face, reflected in the mirror, does not resemble me. A paid biker bodyguard stands at the door. The men are in grey suits, more or less identical, with that look on their faces that they get when you take off your top and they begin to get serious.

I watch them, and I am them: the man who fucks her first (with the satisfaction of the first drive in the new car), the man who fucks her next, maybe the greatest pleasure belonging to the man who fucks her last, when the varnish of aloof woman-ness has worn off her and she

68

*moans like a four-legged animal, her eyes glazed with enduring them,
one after another; they're not gentle like they are with their girlfriends
and wives.*

*Crisp brown, pink, and purple bills pile up in the brandy snifter by
my left shoulder. Getting it, I keep my eye on my money in the mirror, counting how much I'm making as the men take their turns behind
me. Everybody gets what they came for.*

By age seven, I had been turned upside down and probed
by more men than I could count. I spent that year in
Sunnyhill Residential Hospital for Chronically and
Terminally Ill Children. The Hargreaves were a plump,
self-satisfied couple in their middle fifties who taught
Sunday school in the lobby, and every week I was roped
into going by the battleaxe nurses, every last one of whom
detested children. (With the doors locked to visitors,
except during the short visiting hours, these grim women
ran the institution like it was a military prison. At 6
o'clock in the morning, seven days a week, they'd swoop
down and rip off your covers. Then they'd roll you over,
slap you—hard—and you were up. Good morning. This
was the only thing they did with enthusiasm.)
The Hargreaves conducted hymn-sings to syllable-
stress charts printed in a bold, simple hand with a jumbo
felt marker. "Jesus Loves Me" is the only one I can
remember. Even then it struck me as inane. The

Hargreaves were pleasant, well-intentioned souls. They distributed striped peppermints with a free hand—bribes, it seemed to me, but they probably thought of it as positive reinforcement.

When they came to your bed on their rounds, they invited you to "Ask any question you like." I remember asking (more than once) how they could prove the existence of God. A confirmed I'll-believe-it-when-I-see-it subscriber even then, I put no stock in Mrs. Hargreaves's lyrical but evasive answers. ("The beauty of the sunrise should be proof enough for you.") Mr. H. stood silently by, fidgeting with the pipe he would have to wait to be outside to light. He looked, I thought, obscurely troubled.

Sunnyhill. We spent Saturday mornings watching "J.P. Patches" and "Fun-O-Rama" and "Captain Kangaroo" in the day-room, which smelled fetid, with a top note of stale cookies. By the time we arrived Crazy Craig was already in place, tethered to one of the six or so chairs that were bolted to the floor along one wall. He must have been about twelve, with bushy brown hair. I remember him in ripped T-shirt, straining at the white cloth tie, whooping and drooling and cursing, lumpy shit running down both legs. I don't think his parents visited him very often.

Pretty Linda with polio gave me a sugar egg at Christmas. One side had a coloured sugar diorama set in it: a bearded man and a woman with clasped hands bending toward a baby in a cradle. I bit the head off the baby first, grinding it between my teeth like sand until it dissolved.

Dumb Mae was eighteen. She walked slowly, heavily on her enormous feet, and when she talked she sounded like a cow mooing. Wheelchair-bound Paul with the outsized head was the nurses' favourite. We all envied him—his parents were always around. My roommate, Elaine, hardly ever got visited. Neither did the brothers with leprosy or Teddy and Marlene, the native kids.

"Aw, honey, why are you crying?" the nurses would ask Teddy, mussing his hair. I guess Marlene wasn't cute. She got ignored like the rest of us. Those of us who could walk ducked into the janitors' closets a lot, waiting for nurses to pass. I liked the peaceful dimness in the company of the wet string mop, the sleek sponge mop, the squat bulk of the galvanized pail. After night rounds, when I had been wakened and made to take the twenty-two little white pills and the two big fat brown ones, I would creep down the empty halls and into one of these hiding places. Squatting beside the friendly bucket, I would wedge a sponge up under my ribs and rock in the darkness.

I would think about nothing at all, just watch random patterns of rusty red against the black background of my eyelids, the pattern of the pain.

Fragments of the day: watching a nurse bathe little Audrey whose legs ended at the knee and who had three fingers on one hand, two on the other, from playing on the train tracks when the train came. Eating crackers under the sheets with paraplegic Barbara. Being threatened by a nurse that if I didn't eat more I'd have a tube shoved into my stomach via my nose. Hiding in the closet with my battered plush squirrel, wanting to be at home in bed with my mother.

I replayed my dad's visits: his hug, with its familiar wool-sweater feel and smell, the walk around the grounds. On a day in early summer, we held hands and made our way along the mossy path under decrepit apple trees just inside the cracked cement wall.

"... and, covered in garlands of flowering herbs, she climbed into the barge ..."

"What's a barge?"

"A boat. Sort of like a dory. She climbed in and went floating down the river. She was very beautiful, with long golden hair."

"Where did she go?"

"Well, nowhere, really. She died. She'd gone mad, you see." I didn't see. People *got* mad. Was going mad the same thing? Maybe you could die from getting mad. As I was pondering this, he broke into my thoughts by clearing his throat in a way that always precedes bad news. A gnarled bough with green apples drifted before me. I grasped one and twisted it off.

"Sarah kitty, you're mother has asked for a divorce. That means I'll be moving out, but I'll still be nearby." Something shifted under my feet and I stumbled over a broken pull-toy. It lay there grinning up at me as the day grew suddenly dark.

"But I'll still visit you. No need to worry about that."

I saw that I was still clutching the apple. I brought it close to my face and tried to get lost in its roundness, its smooth green skin, the twig of stem and still vital leaf attached.

"I wouldn't eat that."

"Why not?"

"It'll make you sick." I sank into it vengefully, feeling the skin snap under my teeth.

Nine years old. Released from Sunnyhill, back in VGH. They stuck me in the baby ward, across the hall from the incubators while they ran "tests." A nurse came in, leaned over my bed, looked me in the eye and said, "Tomorrow we're going to wheel you to the procedures room, where a six-inch-long needle will be inserted just below your navel," and walked out, leaving me staring at the ceiling for the next several hours.

Around 1 a.m. a perfumy little nurse with sweet lips and strawberry blond hair (I could tell by the glow of her flashlight as she went around the room taking temperatures) came over to my bed.

"Still awake?"

"Yes."

"Is something on your mind?" I told her about the test.

"Well," she said. "You know what I do at times like that?" I waited. I could not imagine her busy little figure

73

on its back in a bed with bars, tucked in so she couldn't move, like a starfish in a holding tank awaiting vivisection. "I pray."

Oh.

"Would you like to pray?"

It's worth a try, I thought. "Okay." I watched her soft-looking lips murmur soundlessly, the tiny gold cross she wore on a slender chain around her white throat resting in her hand. Her fingernails were like tiny pink shells. She smelled of hand lotion, the kind my mother used, a faint scent of almond and hyacinths. Other scents emanated from her hair, her uniform. The minute hand of the clock in the nursery click-clicked, punctuating the silence, the distant whine of babies, far cuter than me, across the hall. I tried closing my eyes. She was praying to Jesus and since I had been raised by parents who believed Jesus was "a nice man but not special like God," she might have been praying to the telephone operator. But really, I knew, it wasn't prayer that I wanted.

I couldn't get adults to talk straight to me about what was wrong. Back in school again, I crept into the nurse's office when she was at lunch and looked it up in her medical encyclopedia:

ULCERATIVE COLITIS: A disease of the immune system in which the body turns on a part of itself, attacking and destroying the lining of the colon, or large intestine. Symptoms are abdominal cramping and bloody diarrhea, attended by dehydration, blood-loss anemia, and other nutritional deficiencies. Cause is unknown, but stress and heredity are thought to be factors. Seventy percent of children with ulcerative colitis are Jewish; it is slightly more common in girls than in boys, often occurring in sisters.

Tuesday, January 3
Smithers

Sherry and I are in her room here at the Bulkley Hotel. We took a two-seater plane in from Terrace. Sherry bussed the hundred or so kilometres to Terrace from her gig at the Prince Rupert Hotel; I came from stripping Kitimat, forty miles south.

Biff, the hotel manager, picked us up at the airstrip and drove us in. With his slouch, tattoos, and strangely colourless curls, Biff looked nothing like the son in *Death of a Salesman.* His hooded eyes frisked Sherry and me as we stood there in the wind waiting for our luggage. I was wearing my black wool jacket and leather pants and cowboy boots; Sherry shivered in a Death Sentence T-shirt untucked over a white denim miniskirt, leg warmers and short white spike-heeled boots. "Don't you even have a windbreaker?" I said. They stared.

I watch her dress for the 4:40. Sitting on her bed in my

$1.50 special, hoping I look good in it and that Lloyd appreciates the money I saved by not buying a thousand-dollar Clyde DuBois off-stage wrap, though goodness knows I want one with every cell of my glamour-seeking being. (Already the Good Wife of Bible fame is showing up in me. She chooseth fresh fish for her husband's delectation, she weaveth fine rugs with her own hands, she weareth cheap off-stage cover-ups that her man may delight in her money, which is no doubt what he is doing right now, sitting at the scrapwood kitchen table eight hundred miles away, with Tod and Fred, rolling a joint in a cloud of pungent smoke.)

I often picture myself swishing across the bar in one of those tiered confections, a jewelled cigarette holder between my perfect nails. For this I'd learn to smoke cigarettes. To inhale through my nostrils, even. Would I get the blue ruffles tipped in white? Or the red ruffles tipped in black? I decide, for the fiftieth time, to have my hair bleached platinum, to go with the blue and white, which goes better with my complexion and besides, I want to be a vision of ladylike delicacy. In any case, I'll get the matching marabou-trimmed satin mules (If only my feet were tiny!), scream into a pillow to make my voice fetchingly dusky, and I'll preface every sentence with, "Honey."

Sherry stands before me in a suedette loincloth, undone, and a beaded bra that she keeps falling out of. Somehow she managed to shuck her skirt and T-shirt without taking off her boots and leg warmers, now scrunched to accentuate the full curves of her calves, her long, perfectly proportioned thighs.

"Can you do this up?" She tilts a hip toward me and I hold back the fringe with my palms and match the velcro with my fingers. She is sucking at a turquoise toke stone with a gold marijuana leaf on it. She hands it to me when I finish and sits down beside me, touching up her tiny, bitten-down nails with Hula Orange. I hold the stone to her mouth when it's her turn.

"How long you been in the business?"

"Two years," I lie. "You?"

"Same."

"So do you, uh, ever fool around with girls?" I think this but I don't say it. She is talking about her boyfriend now, a Satan's Angel named Rolf.

"I met him in Rupert. He comes up to me after the eight o'clock, asks me if I want to shoot some balls. I turned to go and he puts his hand on my face to turn my head, like this." She slaps her own face lightly so it turns her head. "So I'm looking at the pool table and he says, 'Snooker balls, dummy.' But nicely, you know? Just as I'm saying, 'No, really, I'm not very good,' he opens up this little box and says, 'Pretty lady.' Like that. It's got about a gram of coke in it. Well I just stand there for a second, holding it, and when I look up, he's gone. I shut the lid and run after him, to thank him, but all I got was his tail lights. Can you believe it? But he came back later. By Friday," she laughs, "I could hardly walk."

The photo she hands me is of a big guy (six feet four?) with a beard and sunglasses. I look at his big hands in their black leather riding gloves, his narrowness in jeans. Hell, I'd fuck him, too. But what would he say when he saw me naked? (Lloyd stroking my belly and saying, "Some men wouldn't want you, I'm afraid sweetheart."

"What percentage, do you think?" Suddenly anxious, I pictured man after man sneering at me and stalking off in search of his clothes. Lloyd yawned, languorously, considering.

"Oh, I'd say . . . about fifty."

I sat up then, for some reason clutching the sheet to my chest. He pushed it away, climbed on top of me. "But not me, darlin'. I'm wild about you, you know.")

With all those rough hands reaching toward her, all those gleaming eyes and boots and belt buckles, all those ripe bulges, those scents of leather and denim and barely-sheathed knives, what would she want with me? Ever useful Conceal-all is smeared on the bruises I got on my inner thighs gripping the pole in Kitimat. I am hardly a woman's dream.

"Do these look okay with this?" She steps back, twitches on a pair of cheap sunglasses. "I figure I'll take 'em off for my floorshow."

"Let me guess. You're dancing to ZZ Top."

"Uh-huh."

"Don't you have a jungle set to go with your loincloth?"

"Yeah. But I'm sick of 'Wild Thing.' So, do these go?"

"Instant cool," I say. What the hell. Cavewomen didn't wear spike heels, either. She looks at me, quickly, up and down, then gives me another look, longer, and holds it. Then she backs up a few steps, gives me a funny little smile, then grabs her tiger-striped T-dress before splitting. So maybe I'm not a gargoyle. I lie there, not looking at but aware of my reflection in the wavy glass of the down-tilted mirror, which shakes when logging trucks go by, like the Jack Daniels mirror downstairs shakes when fat men cross the bar. My reflection is dusty. A corner of the glass is missing. (In the triangular gap a purple felt tip pen wielded by an anonymous hand has written, "This place is a *hole!!*")

I feel dirty, but not in a good way, not like when men pull their chairs in closer and lean forward, serious and alert. The young ones straddle their chairs and fold their forearms along the top; sometimes I can see individual hairs. Clean-shaven faces, the keen eyes of a bright third-grader watching a gerbil running a race against itself.

Dirty, like something patchy, ill-concealed. Not because I almost made a pass at her, but why. My desire, I realize, is not so much sexual as acquisitive.

Wednesday, January 4
Lying on the waterbed in ripped T,
G-string, and leg warmers, between the 2:00 and 3:15 shows.

"Where are we going?"

"Don't ask. This guy just wants to meet you."

"How much did he pay you?" says Sherry. Biff doesn't answer. At the end of the hall the door is opened by a man in an expensive suit. Something in the way Biff hands us in and then disappears makes me feel like I'm in a movie again. Only this time it's a TV miniseries about women prison inmates. Sherry and I remain against the wall, at a slight angle, like two contestants in a beauty pageant, while the man, having shut the door, leans back in his chair. On the magisterial table before him are an open briefcase, a sheaf of papers, and a tumbler of something golden.

"So," he says. "What are your names?" We give him our stage names. "What are your real names?" We glance at each other and say nothing. He doesn't realize this is a compliment, that we are deferring to his suit and cordovan penny loafers; we could've lied.

"My name's Mark Rhodes," he says. "As you may have guessed, I'm a lawyer." We stiffen. Sherry looks poised to bolt, thinking, no doubt, of the joints in her bureau drawer. "Where are your parents from?" he tries again.

"Chetwynd," says Sherry. A one-horse town in northern B.C.

"Massachussetts," I say. "Why?"

"Just wondering," he says. "Just trying to find out a little more about you. You may leave if you like," he adds, turning to Sherry, who promptly flees.

"I'm not a hooker," I say carefully.

"I can see that."

"You can?"

"Of course. And I can see that you're frightened"—I flinch and harden my mouth—"and lonely like I am. So let's just have some conversation. Won't you sit down?" I back toward the coffee table. My leather pants creak as I sit carefully on one corner. For the next hour I listen to him expound on the nature of psychopaths, a subject with which I am intensely uncomfortable. "I'm here to defend a man whose daughter went off with two young men she met in a park near here. They offered her a drug. She took it and it made her a vegetable. When the father learned what had happened, he murdered the two men. I'm arguing for his acquittal. Look at these."

He hands me a stack of Polaroids. Each photo shows a corpse covered in patches of red, blue, and in places, white, like the decomposing salmon I saw on a sixth grade field trip to a spawning channel. I look up from them to Mark, who is steepling his fingers and staring at his glass.

"What's this?"

He glances up at me and smiles slowly. "Evidence."

He joined me this morning at breakfast, as I sat writing in my journal. I am beginning to enjoy his company. Or, at least, I'm pretty sure he isn't a psychopath. He commented that keeping a journal is a worthwhile thing to do. "Keep writing things down," he told me. Mostly I just sat and listened while he went on about his work, and his wife and mistress. I'm relatively sure he's not going to come on to me. I think he just likes my company. Weird.

"I don't think you have any idea what effect you have on men." He says this slowly, while mopping up egg yolk with his toast. I must have started since he added, "Oh, yes. I've seen you dance, you know. I'm sort of a method actor when I'm on the trail of a prosecution. I hang out in the bar those two vagrants hung out in. Listen to the same cowboy songs on the jukebox. Drink beer although I can't stand it. And watch strippers like yourself, my dear." And then he straightened up and repeated himself: "No, I don't think you have any idea of the effect you have."

"What do you mean?"

"Hard to explain. The other girl is cute, and she certainly has a nice little body, but you've tapped into something much older, something almost mythic. And the fact that you don't understand your power or even that you *have* power—well, it's like talking to a sleepwalker who's out on a ledge. You don't want to wake her for fear she'll startle. Do you know what I mean?" I could feel him watching me closely while pretending not to. I fought off a horrified prickle.

"Nope," I said, getting out my wallet. "And I've got to go get ready. It's my turn for the noon today." But he had already paid the bill. Thanking him, I turned away and found, to my horror, that I'd started to cry.

Dad moved to Israel when I was twelve. His corporeal presence dwindled to the occasional letter, light as a hollow bone, drifting through the slot in a blue Air Mail envelope. Below his signature ("Dad," with a billowy D) came a second signature—the real one?—in impenetrable code. Over time, the English word, the evidence of his relationship to me, grew fainter, while the disembodied Hebrew scratches below darkened.

At fifteen, I began to look for him. I found him, or thought I did, over and over in each man who looked at me a certain way. *I know you*, the look said. *You're rotten or he wouldn't have left you. Wicked. I like that.* Mixed in would be a trace of something I would construe as caring. The man would quote Browning, or discourse on the Impressionists, or confess a fondness for sunsets, or have a beard, and I'd be hooked, reeled in slowly, or simply scooped and tossed in the punt for a quick spearing.

I accepted the hug that would come at the beginning and let the guy play out his preoccupations on my inner organs, waiting patiently for the hug that would come at the end. On the floor of an empty apartment, the reclining front seat of a car banked at the edge of a wood, against the wall of a railyard at night, red light swirling around us, boxcars shunting. I was—I sometimes think I *am*—like the figure on a dock as the ship pulls out. It is a dark ship, like a freighter, and my wreath falls short of the beloved for whom it is intended, falls instead on the oily water, the circle of white flowers shattering on impact, already starting to decompose on the dark tide.

Later, same day

I must pass through the restaurant to get to the bar. I am making my way carefully, trying not to step on the feather boa which I bought to set off the showgirl costume, when a family of four floats up on my left. Mom and Pop are cutting their meat and arguing. Pre-pubescent Junior's gaze is travelling up and down the seams in my stockings; Juniorette's is, for some reason, stuck on my feather garter. Pop catches a whiff (Of what? My cologne, Ennui? Or Junior's testosterone?) looks up, and gets stuck—*zot!*—to my feather boa. Mom, sensing fever running through the ranks, looks up and instantly stiffens.

Her jaws clutch at partly-chewed steak. She's holding her knife in her fist like she's about to knight somebody. And I, why can't I move? I'm looking at the bar door (No Minors Beyond This Point. That rules me out—eighteen is still too young—but hey, they don't even have my real name) and going nowhere. Meanwhile Mom's face is the colour of a poinsettia and she sputters, "This is ... that is ... disgusting. Young woman, have you no modesty?"

I look down for a moment, as if it is some small, neat package, discreetly wrapped, that I am supposed to have with me and have somehow misplaced.

"... Absolutely unacceptable. She should be covered." Pop unsticks his eyes (*thwop!*) and rests them disconsolately on his baked potato that, having been recently unsheathed from its gold foil, is shrinking but still plump.

"I'm going straight to management." As she levers her polka-dotted mass from the chair, I give her a smile that says, "I hope rats nest in your underwear drawer," and a tiny crumpled wave, before swinging through the saloon doors to yelps, catcalls, wolf whistles, somebody whistling with two fingers, somebody blowing me a kiss, somebody grabbing my butt. Yes, once again, it's feeding time at the zoo.

The bouncer is in the hospital with a head wound. Somebody hit him with a bottle that broke. I hear laughter while I'm on-stage. An elderly native woman lurches below and beside me, imitating my act. I know she is not malicious, that this is just her mocking, really quite sharp sense of humour. Nonetheless, I would like to spray her with a giant can of Raid. Damn it, I'm doing my best to be sensuous and alluring on this creaky plywood platform with its mismatched pieces of carpeting, the edges of which I keep tripping on, in front of a barn-sized bar full of bellowing, shrieking, brawling revellers, some of whom are paying attention, some of whom are partly watching the hockey game (turning to look at the tube when the Maple Leafs score a goal or turning to look at me when I make like I'm about to take off my bra), and some of whom, towards the back, are skulking around the pool table in their undershirts and feeding the jukebox so that my music, which I carefully selected for its spellbinding qualities, is just barely audible over Tammy Wynette singing "D-I-V-O-R-C-E."

"I'm not scared."

"Yes you are. You're terrified." Mark Rhodes is holding my two hands in his. And then he steps toward me for a brief hug: my boots toe to toe with his brogues, my jeans against his fine wool trousers, my Dartmouth sweatshirt (courtesy of Bronwyn. She went there to look around when they offered her a scholarship, before she settled on Queen's) against his pinstriped shirt. He is old (mid-fifties?) and not my type. Yet through the fleece, beneath his hands, my shoulder blades feel like the wings of small birds.

It is Wednesday, late afternoon. Lloyd arrives tomorrow. It will be the first time he's joined me on the road, the first time he sees me dance. I'm surprised to find I'm apprehensive. I'm supposed to be excited; instead I feel slightly nauseous with foreboding. I want him to be appalled on my behalf, impressed at what a trooper I am. I want him to throw punches defending my honour. I want to discover in him a rich vein of gallantry but, apart from packing me a bag lunch and several joints when I leave on a twelve-hour bus trip, there hasn't been any sign of it before.

This morning, after the 11:45, Mark and I go for a walk. As we pass cramped-looking, shuttered houses on narrow lots, I dawdle along the slender curb, fantasizing myself as an Olympic gymnast. (Lithe, with the tensile strength of flexed steel, at once commanding and ethereal. After a childhood spent learning the rigours from a grim-faced Romanian coach and a breathtaking gold medal performance, I retire to the B.C. strip circuit, where the costumes are much nicer, there to stun the competition with my three-point dismount from the brass pole.) Mark walks in the gutter, in galoshes like my father used to wear, the button-on kind.

"So Lloyd's coming tomorrow, eh? Shame I won't get to meet him." We cross a muddy field bounded in chain-link, to a pond. Under the grey sky, pregnant with rain, a few ragged-looking white ducks float like cracker crumbs on soup.

"Yeah. You'd probably like him."

"You think?"

"Sure. He's smart and funny and he's a good talker, like you." His hand comes up to cover his mouth as he clears his throat. Somebody else would have planned to steal that watch and sell it, maybe go back to school. "You don't like him, do you? You don't like the sound of him."

"Well. No, actually. I don't." He stops, and I stop and look down at him, trying to glare but I can't. I slept in my makeup last night. Sometimes it's just too much trouble to keep putting it on and taking it off, using a cotton ball dipped in Nivea and Q-tips dipped in special eye-make-up remover, "for that delicate under-eye area." I'm beginning to think I'm delicate all over. I know when I start sleeping in my lipstick and mascara and eyeliner and blusher and sparkle powder and beauty mark it means I'm depressed. But why? I'm making more money this week than I'd make in a month at a restaurant and I doubt I'll get knifed here. After all, Lloyd's coming. He'll protect me.

"I don't know how you can say that," I say feebly.

"Sarah, listen to me. Either he doesn't love you—"

"He does!"

"Are you sure?" I am silent. "Or he hasn't got a clue."

Now, he draws back from our hug. His hotel room is still. The half-empty glasses, the law books, the garment bags that had haunted the closet, all are gone, these last presumably laid flat in the back of his square, fancy-looking car, stuffed with freshly-ironed shirts. His eyes search my face to the faraway bass of Pink Floyd's

"Money" coming up through the floor by the bathroom. Topless by the end of it, Sherry is now probably doing her "six-shooter" routine, tripping forward at an angle to the audience, pretending to twirl guns at her hips. Her head is tilted back, full-blown lips slightly parted. No trace remains of the slightly startled expression she wears off-stage. On-stage, she seems never to be thinking, "What am I doing here?" You would think she came from a long line of dancing girls, or had been bought and sold in the marketplace from an early age, or both. How I envy her apparent singleness of purpose.

"You remind me of Camille." He lifts a ringlet from my forehead, tries to snag it behind my ear, but it springs back, intractable.

"Camille?" My mouth is dry. My eyes feel enormous, my bare throat dangerously open. One quick pass with a razor ... but it is not him I suddenly fear.

I smoke pot constantly these days, to muffle my pounding heart, to slow the leaping phantoms who ambush me on my way to the stage, materializing from the flocked wallpaper with knife or gun. To dissolve the ghosts who wait on their stomachs underneath my bed and behind the shower curtain, listening for my key in the lock after the midnight show. And there is the presence looking out through my eyes in the bathroom mirror. Sometimes, late at night, when I am alone after the last show, I drink German wine and sing every song I know the words to, just to hear the sound of a familiar voice.

"Camille was a dancer, like you. Pretty little thing. She had a habit. She dealt on the side to support it. One day a biker thought she'd ripped him off. He hot-spiked one of her caps and she died."

I have a trick for when I'm in pain. This is what you do: stop your mind. Don't think. Don't wonder, don't hope for it to stop, don't fear it won't. Stay with the moment, as if it were your chosen home. I am doing this now. Trying not to see her stumbling down the hall from her room towards the stage in her sequinned costume. More and more slowly, until crawling. Found later, like a child in a party dress, just outside the walk-in cooler, by the bar manager, irate that she's late, who swings the door wide, hitting her fled skull. (Then realizes, "Oh, Jesus, Jesus," dropping to his knees, "I didn't mean to kill her.")

"She hadn't ripped anybody off. It was a misunderstanding. She was innocent." I look at him the way I can look at my mother, a more total-stranger look than I use for total strangers. He gives me his card. Says, "Keep it somewhere safe."

I don't see him leave. There is a light scent of limes and I am alone in the room, which is ordinary again—the table that looked so magisterial two nights ago turns out to be covered in peeling, wood-grained Mac-Tac. I cannot tell how long I have been standing here.

The woman at the desk in the lobby glowers at me over

her bifocals every time I pass her on the way to the stage. It's a real gauntlet here.

Some gigs you have to walk outside. The other girl and I escort each other. Or, if there is no one, you make a break for it, carrying your shoes in case you have to run. You wear a coat over your costume, or a robe—none of this see-through lace stuff.

Although, to tell the truth, you can slip into old habits. Next thing you know you're traipsing across the parking lot from the hotel to the pub barefoot, stockings balled up in your hands, frozen metal fastenings on your garter belt snapping against your thighs. You try to pick out the broken glass in the headlights of the four by fours pulling in. So many of these places are dead except for show-times. Then you should see the trucks and bikes move in; you'd think they ran on testosterone.

Sometimes I feel the more naked I am—the more shell-less, thornless, and soft spoken—the safer I am. If I play my cards right, smoke enough dope, stop reading, and try not to think, one of these days I might dissolve into the mirrorball lights dappling the room, or into the smoke exhaled from the mouths of the men. In the eyes of the hard-hatted construction workers, the bulletproof cops, the musclebound bartender, I am immobilized. Like a deer exposed in the beam of the Greyhound's headlights, as it slices a ribbon of road through the wooded mountains from here to Burns Lake, from there to Prince George, from there through the sagebrush hills of fruit farm country to the coast. A secret species. A secret country.

At Champagne Harry's you had to walk through the boiler room to get to the stage. I thought sure to God some creep was going to rise up out of the concrete floor and smash my skull against one of the pipes. So much for vulnerability as a defense. The truth is I am a walking potential rape victim. Oh well. Aren't we all? It exhilarates me to walk through the crowded bar after midnight, the only female in the room, wearing one square foot of fabric and a chiffon scarf. A piece of oil-soaked paper strolling through a forest of matches.

"In Quebec I saw a girl get fucked on a pool table. Guys lined up along the sides, watching," Lana Luv told me when we did Kitimat together. I can see it when I close my eyes, as if I were there, dissolved into the shadows behind the jukebox. Faded denim against rounded mahogany corners; a sudden glimpse of delicate limbs against the green of the felt; a thicket of pool cues. Above their greyish undershirts their eyes yellow as wolves'. It's men. It's men who are the secret country.

Saturday, January 7

All week the men have been bugging us to do a double oil show. I don't know where they got this idea but it's now fixed with management—Sherry and I each get paid for an extra show. Since Lloyd got here Thursday, he has been lying around watching TV with boots up on the windowsill, rolling and smoking joint after joint. Now and then he comes down and hangs around at the back. I can see his cowlick from the stage, picked out by the tiffany lamp. ("P—si Cola," it says. There is a jagged hole in one panel.) He's got great muscle definition; those sleeveless undershirts really show it off. But he's scrawny.

What did I think he'd do when he got here? Whatever it was, he hasn't done it.

Sunday

The double oil show was last night. We used Sherry's dropcloth—three-millimetre plastic from Handyman Hardware—and baby oil. I felt ridiculous and so did she, I think. We knew we were supposed to get majorly skin-to-skin, squeeze each other's parts, kiss with our tongues flying. We hadn't touched all week and here we were, eyeing each other up in that dead minute before the music starts. The men were all milling around below like so many pilgrims at a flogging. She gave me a nervous, I-wish-you-weren't-here smile. I eyed her incredible tits and felt like a bantam taking on a Rhode Island Red.

I looked out in the audience and there was Lloyd, one boot up on a table, nonchalantly winding the tape with his pinky. He has one dead eye that always looks elsewhere. According to him, a crazed father of a fifteen-year-old girl emptied a shotgun at him for no apparent reason. When he glanced up and winked it at me a thought broke through the smoke, the shouts, the beer glasses striking each other, and Sherry fidgeting next to me. I had a flash, like remembering a dream, only in this case it was the reverse. Just for a second, I felt real life.

Then the music started. I don't remember much. Of course I'd smoked a coke joint so it was almost painless, but we were so awkward. I would've touched her but she looked terrified that I'd try, and I could just see us covered in oil and grappling in slow motion like a ballroom dance class gone seriously wrong. I thought, no way, and we ended up just doing our usual things side by side as if the other weren't there.

I got through it. I got the extra money. Lloyd is down in the bar right now, buying some indica, which is supposed to be a present for me but I know he'll end up smoking most of it. I told him I'd rather have bath bubbles or a set of watercolour pencils. Or luggage. The zipper on my duffel bag is broken so all my jumbled costumes bulge out. Makes me look like a real class act. (Once, at a bus depot, a stabbed guy was staggering around under the fluorescent lights. He held his shirt up as if he was showing off the wound, but when he came close we could all see the pale pink guts poking through.) But Lloyd said we don't have the money.

"Who's 'we,' paleface?" I said, and he slapped me. He actually slapped me. (Bronwyn, are you out there? You probably wouldn't talk to me now if you saw me.) How did this happen, I thought.

It was three in the afternoon when we left Smithers. Sherry still hadn't moved in her bed. When I looked in, her hair was tangled all over the pillow and she seemed to be snoring.

"Probably all the Talwin I sold her." Biff smiled his crooked smile.

"How many was that?" I asked.

"Oh, I dunno. Ten, twelve." I stared.

"Shouldn't we wake her up? She'll miss her plane if she hasn't already. She's supposed to be in Whitehorse for tomorrow noon." Biff and Lloyd exchanged looks. Lloyd took a suck off his joint and passed it to Biff, who sucked it and gave it back, rocking on the heels of his Air Soles and chuckling in a way I didn't like.

"C'mon, Florence Nightingale," Lloyd said, suddenly efficient. "Move it." He stood and watched while I picked up my luggage and tacked across the lobby with it, stopping to adjust a shoulder strap or to try and get a better grip. Then he darted past me and whipped open the door with a flourish. The pre-oil-show flash came back to me, only this time it stayed. *I hate him*, it went. *I hate him.*

Wednesday, January 25
Kelowna, again
Replacing a stripper who, rumour has it,
walked in, said, "What? No TV?" and walked out.

"You know what you look like from the back when you get down from the stage?" I stop, halfway past the voice, and turn around. It is a crackling voice. An old person. That's why I stopped. In third grade I was a Brownie. I collected merit points for giving up my seat on the bus to old people, a.k.a. "the elderly."

"What?" I ask. I am wearing my turquoise lace Sally Ann robe that has no lining. I am nude underneath. The thin straps of my six-inch red spikes dangle from my fingertips. I had to take them off. I would've broken my neck going into the backbend. I am covered in sweat. Cigarette butts are sticking to the soles of my feet.

"Like this." He tilts his head back and opens his mouth wide at a crooked angle. I stare blankly. The whites of his eyes are yellow, as is the once white stubble around his toothless hole. And then I get it—he is showing me my vagina.

He no longer qualifies as "the elderly."

Somewhere out there—Queen's, to be precise—Bronwyn removes a maroon, leather-bound volume from a library shelf—*History of the Legal Profession in Canada*, say—

and, thumbing through it lightly, moves to an oak table by a window overlooking a treed square. Her fingernails are cut short and clear-polished; her 36Cs demurely sweatered.

"Blondes with big tits are in," Meg says. Often. Bronwyn would be a natural.

At the bar, fat weiners descend and rise, descend and rise on a rotisserie in a glass cage, beside the jar of pickled eggs. From where I stand I can see the bar manager framed in the open door to the walk-in beer fridge. The barmaid's curls bob on his back. They are necking. He has his knee in her groin. A case of Blue hangs from his right arm. The mist swirling around them gives an Andy Warhol's *Frankenstein* effect.

In another corner I can see tattooed Trish sitting on a biker's knee, her blouse unbuttoned to the navel as usual. As I look, the horses and roses and hearts around names crossed out and rewritten, the spider webs and Harleys Rule all run together, like the pattern on the carpet the time some asshole drugged my orange juice and all the bottles on my bureau began to waltz. Her lipstick runs into her eyeshadow and I realize that it's not raining, there is no window, and I am crying.

"What ... what the fuck do you mean?!" I hear myself sputter. "Look, you stupid old geezer, if I didn't have eighteen shows down, eighteen to go and a no-play, no-pay contract I'd walk. I've got splinters in my hands from doing goddamn backbends on that plywood plank of a stage and I'd like to see you get down from that thing and look graceful. I can't help it if there are no stairs, no lights, no mirrors and the tapedeck sounds like its mother mated with a lawnmower ..."

As I refill my lungs a female voice from the back says, "Just do your job."

Suddenly I am making the sort of wounded animal sounds I haven't made since after they saved my life. Any fleeting negative thought—say, puppies being put down at the vet—would bring this forth and it would last for hours. But that was six years ago. I was twelve. Now, I catch myself, mid-trot, in a narrow corridor mirror. There's a sequin sticking to my throat. My mascara has gone south.

We all try for artiness, we girls. We dump a lot of money on our costumes: nurse outfits, French maid outfits, Marilyn outfits, Pocahontas outfits.

"Want to try my new lipstick?," we say to each other, when there are two of us. "Here. Try the blusher and nail polish, too. 'Shell Pink' from the Revlon Weekend-in-Paris collection." We read *Seventeen* magazine. We use mud packs and curl our eyelashes. We do each other's hair. Except for the odd remark ("Your hair's just like Barbie's." "Barbie Bazooms?" "No, silly. Barbie Doll." "Oh, yeah. I had the Barbie Beauty Centre." "Me, too"), we do not reflect on our elaborate grooming, our whirlwind forays through the nearest Shoppers Drug Mart, where we spend what's left after costumes, food, dope, and the Greyhound. Instead, we focus on the way we look in our promo shots, always graceful, always glamorous, or the time a man gave us a hundred dollars "just for looking so good."

On long winter nights before they decided to operate, I read, propping up the book with my non-IV hand, fearful of moving it even a half inch in case the needle should decide to slip from the vein, causing my hand to puff up with saline; I would sit there with it burning until the cry went up "Interstitial!" and the IV team was sent for. Both my arms were punctured and mottled from hand to shoulder, as well as the tops of my feet, where the best veins are. After a few days the older sites turned from blue to the green of tarnished copper, to the yellow of spoiled fruit.

I dwelt with longing on Colette's music hall days, when she was courted by noblemen smitten with her charms, which were fetchingly displayed in her odalisque scenes. I read Isadora Duncan's *My Life* and imagined myself drawn through the streets by a team of white Belgian horses, pink cabbage roses plaited in their manes, after a performance among ruined Roman columns which featured me, dancing barefoot, a solo of aching, transcendent beauty, naked except for the flimsiest gauze.

I ate my Jell-O, swishing it thoughtfully between my teeth, and tried not to keep looking at the glass chamber of the IV with its tiny drops forming and falling like blood from the toe of a hanged man.

Last night: I dream that I am falling, falling. Where does the soul go, under anaesthetic? On dark afternoons in dressing rooms, I stand before the mirror, sponging foundation makeup on my scar. You'd be surprised what you can't see from the audience.

I have had myself photographed in my two favourite costumes. One I call Cowboy Princess and the other, Stripping Fairy. Cowboy Princess has a tiara and pink boots; Fairy has wings. They look a little like dragonfly wings—I had some trouble with the wire. Anyway, the photos are supposed to be promo shots but I sent copies to my friends, my mother, and my dad at the last address I have for him. You never know when you might be seeing someone for the last time.

Now I am stumbling, almost falling, and the hotel carpeting (black squares on red, purple and blue) is buckling and heaving like it's going to rise up and engulf me.

Nikki, the other dancer, comes out in the hall. At first

she just hangs in the doorway, dressed in her biker set, which is not too far off from her real life: short shorts, black rubber spikes to mid-thigh, heavy eye-liner, lots of jangly jewelry.

"Say, kid, you plastered?" Her voice is deep and hoarse. I stumble. She comes toward me, takes my elbows. "Tabitha? Hey, c'mon now. What's—?"

Over her shoulder I can see the four members of the band that's playing the late nights this week. (One of them has a crush on me. When I arrived, crossing the bar in my black leather pants to ask where to put my luggage, he and the drummer were setting up their amps.

"Psst." I saw him nudge his buddy. "Look at her eyes." I look in the mirror as soon as I get to my room but I can't see anything special). They duck their heads shyly when I pass them on my way to the stage, smile and say hello in the coffee shop where I'm eating my pancakes. Now they look up, shaking their long hair back from their ears as if listening. The slender fingers of the guitarist are frozen above his strings.

I, too, have gone rigid, and so has Nikki, behind me. I can feel the steady thub-dup, thub-dup of her heart between my shoulder blades. Down the corridor, a figure is approaching.

"Tab? Little Tabby? Is that your name? Hey, I didn't mean to make you cry. When I said just do your job I didn't mean it like that ..." She gets closer, gets bigger and I can see she's platinum blond and very big—obese, actually. Her sweatshirt has an iron-on picture on it, cartoon captioned. It probably says something like "Beer Drinkers Get More Head" but I am past reading.

Now she is hulking over me, saying something. She stretches out her arm for me to shake her hand. I glance around wildly. I feel as if I am underwater. I find that I am trembling. I try to stop. To tremble is to look like prey. I stand there, swaying, as one second bleeds imperceptibly into the next. And then, as if from a long way off, I hear a male voice, polite but firm.

"No," it says. "She doesn't want to talk to you. I think you'd better leave." Nikki clasps me tight around the waist, lays her cheek on mine. The four young men close in around us like an oyster embracing two pearls.

Friday, January 27

"Sweetheart," says Lloyd. The phone line crackles. "Listen carefully. There's a house I want us to move to. It will be great for my business." He's talking about the closet full of marijuana plants growing under mixed spectrum fluorescents against the day I've finally worked enough shows to buy us halides.

"Sleep comes down." I have this sentence in my notebook, between a list of possible floor show songs and "six prs red stckgs w blk seams." I can't remember why I wrote it, or when. These days I feel like I'm looking through a shower curtain, the clear plastic kind. Sleep comes down, a kind of protective dressing, and when life starts seeping through the gauze, I light another joint.

Now, over the phone, I listen to him go on and on about some house out on some highway.

"... concrete-floored carport. You'll love it," he's saying. "Please, sweetie? It's only a little more than twice the rent we're paying now." I'm paying. But who's counting? (As they used to say at faculty sherry parties, as one or another drunken prof reached for the decanter. I'd be wearing a tartan jumper and circulating with a tray of chicken livers wrapped in bacon. When no one was looking, I ate the bacon and dropped the livers into the umbrella stand.)

My feet are killing me. It's six shows a day here and I just got off number five. Holding the receiver against my shoulder, I ease off one rhinestoned spike, then the other, and stand on each leg by turn while I rub the opposite foot. I hear, "Git, git git," and "Yeeeehaw!" from the bar as Nikki gets underway with her cowgirl set, which is always a big hit. (She wears nothing on the bottom but her sparkle-studded chaps, does rope tricks with her lariat, and never takes her hat off. "On a good night," she tells me, "I can knock a man's cigarette out of his mouth at fifteen feet.")

"Is there an apple tree?" I always wanted to wake up in an attic bedroom with an apple tree blossoming outside those windows with the little tiny diamond panes and a blue and white jug holding pussy willows. Just like Anne of Green Gables.

"Well, no ..."

"No? Lloyd? Why don't you wait till I get home?"

"Can't wait. Place'll be gone. But now I think of it, there might be an apple tree. Fact, I'm almost sure there is." Nikki is on her last song already. I have ten minutes in which to change, rewind a tape, and touch up my make-up.

"Fine," I say. My voice comes out sounding like a recording. "Whatever."

Saturday, January 28

Nikki calls me from the bathroom.

"Honey, will you look at this." She points to some red sequins on the tile floor. "I do believe my period's here." It is one of those dark fish-tank days with the rain bubbling on the roof outside. Our laughter mixes with the half dark of the rain, and faint voices from the TV.

"But seriously," she adds, swinging a lace-up gladiator spike onto the sink. While she trims the pink tampon string so it doesn't show on her spreads, it occurs to me I haven't had to do that since ... when? Shit. Who knows? I've three weeks left on my tour. Lloyd says we need the money since the friends of his who are staying there (How many are there?) are all on welfare and "can't chip in much." And though both Tod and Fred are permanent fixtures, they don't sleep there. I have to keep going.

When I finally get back to the coast I am zombified with fatigue. The house is on the Dollarton Highway, just outside North Vancouver. Even in the falling dark I can see it isn't Green Gables. The cab pulls out of the drive and I stagger through the tangled grass and brambles to the graffiti'd boards over the basement windows, up the stairs and in the door, dropping my luggage on the peeling hall lino, which is already covered with sneakers and a layer of dope roaches.

I follow the pounding bass to the living room. Lloyd and Tod and Fred and some guys I don't know are standing around drinking, and I know instinctively there is no bed upstairs, no pussy willows for miles, and the vague, romantic scene I'd envisioned—him and me on stepladders, wallpapering the cute attic rooms ("Isn't this wonderful, honey? Our new house" "Sure is")—is never going to transpire.

Just inside the door, I drop to my knees and collapse against the furthest wall, since there is no furniture, and pull my coat over me. Somebody kicks at my hair, "playfully."

"C'mon, Sarah. Don't be a spoilsport." I hear glasses clink, the shiver of shifting ice and dimly, as if through a misty shower curtain, I see Lloyd and Tod and Fred, their faces turned toward me, distorted as through a drop of water. Fred raises a glass in mock salute. And then, mercifully, sleep comes down.

It turns out I'm fourteen weeks gone. While I am sitting on the examining table doing up my shirt my pediatrician, grey-haired now, pulls a chair up to me and sighs. "Sarah. Why did you wait so long to come and see me? Another week and you would've had to have it. As it is, I'm going to have to pull some strings—'extenuating health circumstances, possibly life-threatening' etc." I pull the skin off my left thumb cuticle. "Sarah, do you want to talk?" A nurse comes in and rinses something at the sink with its old-fashioned taps. I watch bloody water swirl down the drain like grenadine flecked with fruit.

A man in dark glasses sits on a milk crate in the living room.

"I'll front you the whole set-up," he tells Lloyd. His voice is muffled and gravelly, as if he's talking through a handkerchief. I think of Leon Redbone. "Lights, troughs, soilless medium. You say the room has a drain in the floor?" Lloyd nods. "It's very low risk," says just-call-me-Charles. "By the third crop you'll own the whole rig outright.

After that, pure profit." He chuckles. "Except for my cut, of course."

His lady (as in, "... and this is my lady") lounges beside him, one hand on the jewelled collar of a small, fluffy dog. She has the kind of hair usually likened to cornsilk. I look around at the banged-up couch, the beer bottles and dirty socks, the old cable spool with its litter of rolling papers and blackened butter-knives. In the mirror image of the scene, in the sliding glass door, our eyes meet briefly, accidentally. Quickly, I look away. She sends me a faint, cool smile, then gazes off without looking at any of us again.

I can feel the heat coming closer.

In the middle of the night, I hear a car pull into the driveway. Then silence, a slam, crunch, crunch and it's gone, its tail lights washing over the ceiling like red and white water, the wake of a fantail fish.

Tod and Fred are giggling in a corner. Fred never goes anywhere without his styling brush. Lloyd is asleep on the couch. Blues are coming from the kitchen, smoke and voices. I tiptoe across to Lloyd, bend down and tickle him behind his ear, thinking he might wake up and kiss me, like they do in the movies. Like he used to when we were first living together in the apartment over the deli. He leaps up and kicks me in the stomach. I fall. Tod and Fred scamper out to the balcony. All over the house I hear footsteps dispersing like giant cockroaches when a light comes on. Lloyd and I stare at each other across the couch.

"Why?" But it comes out a whisper. I shake my head slowly, holding back tears.

Lloyd shrugs. "You woke me up."

We continue to stare.

"I'm a man," sings Muddy Waters from the kitchen.

I walk in the woods between the house and the highway. A washer and dryer lie rusting, their little metal feet pointing skyward. Beneath the toes of Bronwyn's old cowboy boots the rotted leaves breathe out damp. I am stepping on their tiny veins, crushing their tiny lungs. The sky comes through the pines in splintered bursts. I wander, kicking toadstools, my gloveless hands tucked up my sleeve.

I want you to understand. I can't give you what you need. I don't have enough love. It's all I can do to look after myself. So you'll have to go back. Find someone else. Almost anyone would be better. It's strange, feeling someone has set up housekeeping inside me.

It is still dark out when the alarm goes off.

"Lloyd," I whisper, but he doesn't move. I don't tickle

him behind the ear. "Lloyd," I say louder. He opens his eyes.

"What?"

"Wake up. We have to go in an hour."

"What the fuck?" He stretches. "Oh, yeah. Shit." Then he opens his eyes—his eye—and fixes it on me. I am shivering in my nightgown. This big house is always cold. I miss the old apartment with the warm-eyed Italian men in the street below. ("For you, *signorina*." The extra slice of sausage or the extra scoop of ice cream. In the split second between the compliment and my smile back, I'd feel like a genuine Beautiful Woman.

"Beautiful Women intimidate me," Lloyd once said when we were sitting around, him and Tod and Fred and me around the spool with its scars from hot-knifing hash.

"What am I?"

"You?" They watched as he appraised me, leaning back in his undershirt and jeans. "You're just an ordinary pretty girl.") Now he sits up. I go to put my arms around him and he shoves me away.

"Naw. Naw, don't touch me." He looks around the room, slowly, and then at me, slowly, up and down. "Look at yourself," he says softly. "You make me sick. And look at this room, will you? You never do any work around here." I start to cry. I cannot believe this is happening. And then he's yelling.

"Clean it up. You stupid, lazy bitch." And I am creeping around the room, picking up objects and trying to focus on them, trying to clean up, but sniffling, and then sobbing, all the time him sitting on the edge of the bed with his fingers laced behind his head, watching me slowly, his eyes yellow like a lizard's. There is a sudden movement across the hall, as of someone frozen coming back to life, then footsteps into the bathroom and the sound of the shower. Lloyd shoves past me for the kitchen. Dressed, and still crying, I end up in the basement bathroom with the light out, curled on the floor, resting my head against the toilet. Then I pull myself together and head up to the kitchen phone.

"Mom?" I haven't spoken to her in a year, since she moved to Victoria, on Vancouver Island. "I'm having an abortion. Today. At 9 o'clock."

"I'll call in sick and catch an early ferry. I'll meet you there."

I am, as they say in books, flooded with relief.

On the way to the clinic the taxi passes a giant, blue-eyed, pink-cheeked baby boy crawling across a billboard. "One Good Reason Not to Have an Abortion," it says. I want to put up a billboard across the street showing my straight-A report cards, my National Essay Contest award notice, my skinny little body, my lost eyes. In the background I'd have Lloyd like he was this morning, a fine figure of a man hunkering over a bowl of cornflakes beside a stack of porn magazines and a package of rolling papers. The billboard would be ripped down the middle, torn in two, the shreds flapping in the wind created by the cars going by: cars bearing ordinary people to schools, well-lit offices, warm houses with real furniture. Instead, I turn my head.

Lying in a bed with bars, covered in knit hospital blankets, pale yellow, baby blue, with an IV in my arm and my mother in the waiting room reading Barbara Pym, I feel delivered.

"I've come to explain the procedure to you," says a nurse. She has red hair and an Australian accent. Sharp features, a scatter of freckles, friendly hazel eyes. "Then, if you want to discuss birth control or you have any questions, that's what I'm here for." But I know what happened. Home between gigs, I took out my cervical cap too early one night. For that I almost paid with my future.

They start the anaesthetic drip as I lie on the operating table, looking up at the doctors and nurses, six or seven masked, gowned figures looking down at me, bright lights in my eyes and the gleam, everywhere, the gleam of chrome. The room spins. I must look terrified because suddenly the nurse nearest me bends over and lays her body on top of mine, her cheek against mine, and then someone does something to the IV and I am in the recovery room. In my memory, she is faceless. But her gift remains. That sudden gesture, like wings enfolding.

My mother came and got me from Outpatients.

"Lloyd was there," she told me later, "with an old Rambler, wanting to take you back to the East Side. I was polite but firm. I told him no." The red-haired nurse helped bundle me into the backseat of Mom's raspberry-coloured Honda, made cozy with flannel sheets, a pillow shaped like a cat, and the afghan she knitted the winter I was thirteen, the winter my resentment toward her froze into a solid snowball. She set a tin of kitten-shaped short-breads near me, and a thermos of tea in case I should wake up during the ferry ride from Vancouver to Victoria, on Vancouver Island. She laid a hot water bottle at my feet.

The ferry ride across the Strait of Georgia is not quite as scenic as the Inside Passage but it's close. I usually jump when the foghorn sounds, signalling the entry to Active Pass. You can see bald eagles in the lodgepole pines of the headlands, narrowed in, dense and mysterious. I like to stand on the car deck, as near to the water as possible, and scan the surface of the sea. Sometimes it's a dark, foaming jade green, but usually it's flat and silver-grey like a foil gum wrapper balled up and smoothed out by the hand of an anxious teenager. The cars behind me are dead, their nerves severed by the turn of a key. I stare and stare, and try to feel the life below me, the life out there. I imagine what it would be like if the bottom of the ferry were glass. What silver forms would flash in the shifting, murky light. What dark bodies weave among the kelp whose long fronds shimmy and sway like belly dancers.

The ship carries us all: me, my vacuumed womb restored to its original pristine condition; the car, awaiting redemption at a touch; my mother, guarding me in the passenger seat (where she has more room) restlessly riffling *Better Homes and Gardens* in search of the Perfect Sugar Cookie. The ship's dark aorta pumps and empties, fills with new blood and flushes again. Seen in miniature, here we'd be: two tiny figures in a matchbox car, inside a perfect, intricate seagoing vessel. Like the painted wooden doll on my mother's coffee table, who smiles although her middle's been cut with a bandsaw. Pull her apart and there's another, almost identical doll, inside. She, too, has been maimed and smiles. Pull *her* apart and there's another, identical, inside, until the whole thing ends (or begins again) with a baby. The only difference here is that if you pull me apart, I am empty, empty, and you are left with two halves of a person who's been bisected for nothing.

Grey seagulls grip the railings. With their dirty yellow feet and puffed-up strut, they look pompous and disreputable, like senators. But when they take wing they are beautiful. Dark bodies ply the silken seas below us. All around us out there inarticulate spirits make themselves known to us, then vanish. Who is to say what any of us will remember?

I lie on the fold-out couch in my mother's one-bedroom apartment, drifting in and out of dreams. She starts me on chicken soup, works me up to bagels with cream cheese, slices of apple strudel. Returned from work, she tucks me up in an afghan beside her on the couch and we watch the 6 o'clock news. During the long silent days I read magazines full of happy homemakers and their cookie recipes. ("My family simply *adores* these Walnut Toffee Bars," says Bev M., mother of four.") And then the phone rings.

"Sarah?" It's Lloyd. "I got busted. I'm in jail." I close my eyes and lie back on the pillow. Red and white lights like water play across the inside of my lids.

"Will I be busted, too?"

"No. Listen, Sarah. You know that lawyer guy you met? You said he kind of liked you? Give him a call, will you? For me. Use your influence with him. See if he'll help me out."

"Okay," Mark sighs. "But for God's sake, Sarah. Leave the guy."

On the way out I pause in my mother's doorway. She is sitting in bed, propped up on pillows. The phone cord snakes across the white chenille bedspread to her mouth.

"Rhodes," she is saying. "R-h-o-d-e-s." She looks me up and down, smiling. "No. No money changed hands." Then, "Well, I'm glad you think so. Really? You think …?

Eventually she hangs up. "That was Lilah. Sarah, Lilah was just pointing out that this lawyer fellow must like you. She says the work he's done for you could be worth as much as ten thousand dollars. Imagine! That's like a diamond necklace." She gazes hopefully at the small mounds made by her feet in the bedclothes. I stripped to "Pearl Necklace" last week at a stag at a Ramada Inn. It's not about pearls at all but the nacreous nectar of a man. I shift uneasily, for the room is suddenly peopled with my mother's hopes.

There, by her desk, is cousin Raina. She is standing under a wedding canopy, next to Stan, slender and pale like the groom in "Matchmaker, Matchmaker." She is a radiant, waxing moon, eager to repopulate the state of Israel from her loins. Right here in front of me, wading through the bed as through a cotton sea, is Naomi Weisenberg. I have never seen her, but I have heard about her brilliant success as a neurologist from my mother, and here she is, shading her eyes, looking through the walls for something or someone. She is the daughter of Ora, my mother's best friend from college.

"We had so much in common." All my mother's daydream sighs stir the air and settle at my feet, pecking lightly at the varnished wood floor as if it were a grassy lawn. "But Ora had the good fortune to marry Bud."

"What kind of a name is Bud?" I once asked her.

"It's a nickname. His real name is Manley." Honestly. Anyway, ol' Bud never wandered off on his family. Unlike my father, Bud had an unlimited devotional attention span. He remained at home in their New York brownstone, coddling eggs for Ora as her arthritis advanced, walking slowly beside her in Central Park on crisp November days. On my birthdays, while I was shuffling through leaves trying not to remember Dad, Bud was laying a lap robe around his wife's knees while an amount the size of her rent check was being silently deposited in Naomi's account.

As I watch, Naomi, in a tweed skirt and one of those awful blouses with the big floppy bows, fades, and here is Bud, rising out of the chenille waves, juggling glass spheres. I look closer. Each contains, it appears, a tiny female doll. He hurls them into orbit confidently, catches them with care. His movements are unhurried. He looks neither young nor old; his expression is placid, maybe a little sad.

"Honey, are you all right?" The carnival (or whatever it was) vanishes. Outside somewhere a car door closes. A motor starts up and the car pulls out, displaced by silence as if it had never existed. I am my own *doppelgänger*, fidgeting in my Dartmouth sweatshirt. An unsatisfactory substitute for the daughter I might have been.

"I'm fine," I say. Once, in remission, I went on a hospital field trip to some giant water slides. Looking in my mother's eyes is like this. I want to let go and be carried away. I also want to stay gripping the sides, holding against the current, and remain so, forever.

"Sweetheart, if I may say so, you don't look fine to me."

"What do you know," I say, as rudely as possible, and rush forward, fists clenched, to stand panting beside her bed, torn. And then I whirl and am gone.

Friday, February 24
Victoria, still

Sleeping in the front room of her apartment, filled with newspapers, read and unread, underfoot the soft carpet with its familiar pattern, convolvulus.

Last night she told me a story about something that happened recently just down the road from her at the marine park. The young woman whose job it was to feed the whales had fallen into the pool with them and drowned.

"They took her out to the middle of the pool," she said, "to play with her, as if she were prey they'd caught in the wild." The local, fish-eating killer whales are different from the transients. Whereas the local pods are organized around the family unit—typically, a mother and her sons—the transient whale swims alone, probing cold corridors for larger prey, such as a sea lion cub, which it will drag out to open water and brutalize, sometimes for hours, before eating it.

I am down at the bay this morning, having passed mallards and wood ducks congregating under the Garry oaks, to squat here on the sand and watch the waves splashing this rock, as if trying to work it clean. She was the pride of the community, my mother had said, a crack biology student, a national-level swimmer.

("I overheard an old woman in the fish shop say, 'Looking at her, you would have thought she cast no shadow.'")

They are empty, these waves, where last summer they held small jellyfish, each about the size of a poached egg and clear as plastic, clear as glass. I find I cannot stop the tape loop. It ran until I fell asleep and it runs now:

The sun glinting off turquoise. The rounded noses and angled fins breaking the surface of the water. The one false move. The tread that didn't live up to the manufacturers' assurances, the deck paint worn smooth under years of trainers' feet.

The stumble. Was it a failure of traction between shoe and concrete? Or was it something different: an ankle suddenly buckling or somehow tripping over her feet or the bucket that contained the herrings?

The cry. There must have been one. Did the shrieking of gulls, hanging around for scraps of fish, drown it out? Her thoughts. Did she think at first they were coming to rescue her? Did her mind retrieve stories of dolphins cavorting with swimmers? Or, more likely, of the well-known behaviour of whales when one of their own is hurt? Swooping underneath the wounded and surfacing, so that the invalid is borne aloft on the waves? In those her last moments did she comprehend through some inchoate telepathy their thoughts, their glee or indifference?

The massive, rounded, black and white forms moving in an unaccustomed pattern through the turquoise, converging on a doll-like form floating on the surface of the water and that water surrounding it, in an ever-increasing area, beginning to turn a deep, rich red.

Saturday, February 25
Packing.

When I open my eyes in the morning at Mom's, I think at first I am seeing wave patterns on the ceiling. But it is only her bamboo blinds, billowing and receding in the wind that twitches the leaves in the gutters.

My mother, sprightly in her bright blue jumpsuit and tennies, pours out freshly squeezed orange juice, sets it at my place next to a dish of *crème caramel*: my favourite breakfast. I am still in bed. She is on her way out to her water-wings class. It's really quite cute. I watched one once: grandmotherly types with rosy faces, glowing from the exertion, doing graceful, flipperlike movements with empty bleach bottles.

Is this the woman who once told me she contemplated suicide when she was pregnant with me? Is this voice, uplifted in "Red River Valley," this voice that reminds me of the bell-shaped flowers of the morning glory, the same voice that, twisted like catgut, spat out the names of my father and my father's fathers?

Squatting on the dining room floor, the fire unlit, the house cold, only the pilot light in the stove keeping the faith, burning with a low, blue, wintry flame. In the throes of divorce, the man of her dreams having turned out to be a spoiled child, all her dreams of wholeness shipwrecked on the shoal of reality. She must have been desolate.

"You were talking to yourself in your sleep last night."

"Oh? What did I say?"

"You said, 'Something is swallowing me.' Do you remember the dream?" She is looking into my face, concerned. But I remember nothing of the dream. I try and chase it but I can't bring it back.

When I leave my mother's apartment, I know I won't return.

Wednesday, March 8
Castlegar

Sitting in the café, waiting for my omelette. (Grateful for the warmly-smiling waitress: attitudes from female hotel staff always very mixed.) It's snowing hard. Yesterday the other dancer and I went walking, poking through stores, she looking for reading material since her TV only gets two channels. Mine gets none but I don't care.

She picks up *Playboy* and *Penthouse*, and we leaf through them, checking out tit jobs, dye jobs, skimpy little costumes.

"Nice boots," says Kris.

"Nice tits."

"These are good, too." Reaching for *Modern Romance* and *True Story*. She buys one, along with a *National Enquirer*. I check out something called *Entrepreneur*.

"I am nothing," I think, "if not an entrepreneur." She looks at heavy metal magazines, lingering over promotional photos of pouting youths with long, questionably-clean hair, razor stubble over their baby fat. Most of them look as if it hasn't been long since they lay around their mothers' houses emptying the fridge and refusing to pick up their socks.

"Nice tattoos." She buys a magazine filled with men and women, mostly middle aged, all covered in ink. In the faces of the women, a kind of valiant resignation, as if to say, "This is my only mark of worth. Without it, no one would look at me." I once saw a woman on the cover of *National Geographic*. Her neck was stretched to about a foot with a series of elaborately painted rings. These, the text explained, were a mark of beauty. But, it added, if for some reason her husband suspected her of adultery, he could remove them with a stroke of his wrist; she would suffocate instantly.

Later, same day

Last night. Watching her dress for the 10 o'clock. She puts on her little silver sequinned jacket and miniskirt with matching T-bar, G-string, and fingerless gloves. Sprays on perfume lavishly, as if it were that new-car scent you buy in a can.

"And this asshole says, 'How 'bout a big kiss for my

friend here? He's getting married tomorrow.' I just looked his friend up and down like this, said 'sucker,' and walked away."

Kris also likes to look at *Brides* magazine. She likes the pretty white dresses, the clever little shoes with matching gloves. At first I thought this represented an anomaly in her position but now, having thought about it, I'm not so sure.

Yesterday we went to the boutique across from the hotel, an eclectic shop such as you would only find in a small town, selling grad formals, bridal gowns, assorted party dresses and, in a side room, the exotic lingerie advertised outside. I assumed we were cruising for stuff to wear in our acts, but she went straight to the rack of wedding dresses and picked out one she felt was the prettiest, with a lot of ruffles in the back that must have been a train, and a lot of opalescent sequins on the front. She wanted to try on one of the headpieces, I could see that.

"Do you think it would look dumb on me?"

"Dumb! Of course not," I said, surprised and obscurely moved by her diffidence. "Here. Is this the one you like?" She put it on and I helped her straighten it for the best effect. "You're beautiful."

"You think so?"

"Definitely." I stood back. She was looking at me almost shyly, with the ghost of a new beauty hanging about her face like a veil, when the saleswoman stepped between us and offered her a hand mirror and she turned her back to me, so that even if I'd wanted to, I couldn't intercept the look she exchanged with her bride self.

Shifting on the deep pile carpet of the fitting salon I felt awkward, embarrassed in the presence of so many deep dreams. Across the room a plain, rather heavily-upholstered girl was trying to squeeze into an improbable creation in pink chiffon. I thought of something my mother told me, about an exercise at a workshop she attended with other people from the "helping professions."

"We formed a circle. One at a time, we went around and whispered in the others' ears that thing—that *one thing*—that would have made a difference in our lives to have heard more often or even ..." She paused. "... just once." I waited. I knew she would tell me what she had said. I wanted to know and I dreaded finding out.

"One woman actually whispered in my ear, 'You're prettier than Etta May and you always were.' Can you imagine?" She took a sip of her Earl Grey and cut a half slice of banana loaf in half again. I knew she would eat first one piece and then the other; she always did.

"And ... what did you say?" My voice came out a throaty whisper in the silent apartment. A rose-scented geranium stirred in a breeze from Oak Bay Avenue. Across the street, a seagull landed on a balcony.

"I said, 'You're smart and beautiful and I love you.'"

Another time she told me, "I grew up with an image in my mind of a baby lying in an icy puddle." She repeated this, for emphasis, in case I had failed to photograph it the first time, so that now it is lodged in *my* mental file, too, and forms in front of me at strange times, like crossing the slushy street with Kris, from the boutique back to the hotel. (Joking to her, "Easy does it. You want to survive all the loonies in the bar only to get mowed down by a moron in a Chevrolet?" She giggles; I've caught her off guard).

Went out for a walk earlier. Coming in from the snow I see Kris on-stage, her legs spread like a child in a sandbox, wearing only a G-string and a teasing smirk. She reaches up to pull the pins out of her hair and it ripples over her hands like tiny pink garter snakes under the coloured light. I think suddenly of the Liddle Kiddles my sisters had. Each doll had a name like "Apple Blossom," "Sweetbriar," or "Eglantina," and was scented to match. When you opened the coloured glass case you would smell her sweet perfume and be enchanted by her hair. It would be periwinkle or mauve, or, I seem to remember, a kind of aqueous green, like seaweed or bottleglass, the kind you find washed up on the beach, sharp edges worn smooth. The men, pretending boredom, are very still. As she slips off her G-string and begins the series of fluid movements that make up her floor show, I slip out and head for my room. The music follows me.

"I told my mom I'm dancing," said Kris.

"Oh, yeah. What did she say?"

"She said, 'You're a fuckin' whore and I don't ever want to see your face again.'" She was brushing her hair back from her pale face as she spoke. Now she turned and gave me a strange smile before running past me, rounding the stairwell, her sneakered footsteps fading with her descent.

We have studiously avoided asking each other questions we don't like being asked, like, "How old are you?" and "How much are they paying you?" This morning in the drugstore, though, she was looking at a Chinese horoscope: Year of the Rooster, Dog, etc. Each animal was followed by some bold-face dates, quite disparate.

"Year of the Rooster," she began, and I knew she was twenty-one. "Frequently a loner, yet you often appear to others as adventurous."

"Are you a loner?" I asked.

"Uh-huh." She flipped the magazine shut and got in line. I hung around, not in the queue since I wasn't buying, reading the tabloid headlines. I sidled up to her and murmured,

"Coma Victim Reports: 'I Went to Heaven and Met Elvis.'" She laughed out loud, then.

Still snowing. Twenty-five shows down, five to go. In the café again, keeping Kris company since I'm not hungry. The waitress has just taken her order.

"Sometimes," says Kris, sitting forward, "I have this crazy fear that someone's gonna walk in and shoot me, right there in the bar, in the middle of my show. Bang! It would be so easy, you know? Walk in, put a bullet in me, turn around, walk out." I recognize this one. "I've never told anyone," she adds. "A friend of mine was killed this past summer. In Port Hardy. That's why I won't go there."

I've danced both Port Hardy bars. The Thunderbird and the Seagate are cavernous, dilapidated bars with no railings around the stages, much less brass poles to do tricks on. The stage in each place is covered in filthy red shag carpeting; you wouldn't even think of doing the splits on it with its reek of smoke and stale beer and baby oil (from some girls' oil shows—who knew how far back?) and the objects enmeshed in it: cigarette butts, hairpins, feathers, sequins, fake fingernails. You bring your own rug to spread at the start of the last song for your floor moves. You take a lot of baths.

"This guy was following her. She didn't encourage him at all. Kept saying, 'Get lost. Leave me alone ...'" She trailed off unhappily.

"So what happened?"

"He waited till the middle of the night, then broke into

126

her room. He broke a leg off the bed and … I can't say what he did to her before she died." She finished the sentence quickly, under her breath, then seemed to spit the next words. "They said he cut her in half. They had to identify her by her dental work. Shit," she added suddenly. "She wasn't even eighteen."

The waitress pours her more coffee, then brings a plate of hotcakes, a small brown farm egg in a stainless steel cup alongside, and bustles off.

"They're nice here," says Kris, snapping her gum then taking it from her mouth and molding it to the end of her fork. "Some places they treat you like you're lower than dogshit, don't they? Like you're not even human." I am still watching her for traces of—what? Fear? To see if she feels in the front of her mind that what happened in Port Hardy can happen anywhere. But her face is closed, even cheerful as she neatly lops the top off her egg and plunges in with her spoon.

Late night, Sunday, April 24
On the Greyhound, having just left Hope.

I let myself into the house on the highway. It is even more of a disaster than usual. The cops have turned every drawer onto the floor. An eggbeater lies tangled with a nutcracker, as if they have been in a brawl. A ball of string leaves loopy duodenal trails around boxes of cookies mice

127

have got into. A fan of nude photos of me taken by Lloyd lies in the middle of the kitchen table, having been placed carefully, intentionally, like a triumphant poker hand, by a cop.

Except for the distant whisper of cars on the highway, no sound accompanies me as I extract my few belongings: a Swiss army knife, a marble peach, my fairy book, my clothes. The house is ringingly empty. Only Lloyd's whereabouts are certain. He is in jail. Apart from the key, I leave only a trail of absence, like a signature erased.

Part Two

Eight months later

The door is opened by a woman in a house dress and apron. Martha. (I am a Christmas present for her father-in-law, from his long-ago boss and legion buddy. This is in Cloverdale, a semi-rural suburb of Vancouver. By day, I'm on at the Blueboy in Vancouver this week, lolling around backstage with Temper Tantrum and Wildkatt, like three bitchy harem slaves.) Martha is smiling warmly, as if expecting me to try and sell her Girl Guide cookies. Then, as her eyes adjust, her smile slips, like glasses falling off a face. She recovers, but not altogether. "Just through here."

She takes my coat and leads me into a biggish room containing about twenty people, some of whom are seated around a cleared space. Small flames lick the ceramic logs in the gas fireplace. Other family members are standing around a paper-covered table. When I walk in, the noise dims to a hush.

"I bought a pink lightbulb for this little lamp here," she says. "Will that be okay?" Someone flicks off the overhead light.

"I'm sure it will be fine," I say, dropping my robe. I can feel the testosterone beginning to lap around my ankles in little waves, and something else (the gazes of the women?), nibbling, like little sharp-teethed fish.

"We just have our den tape player. I hope that's okay."

"Fine," I say again. And then someone takes my tape, pops it in, and I'm off, twirling and shimmying—or trying to. Dancing spike-heeled in deep pile shag is like those dreams where you try to run but can't move. I end up lifting my feet a lot, giving a rather too wholesome barefoot-in-the-dew effect. As I free my tits, I sense the hands of the female relatives frozen over the bowls of cheese curls and clam dip.

And there I am, rolling around on the wall-to-wall, preparing to artfully expose my pussy in front of the slip-covered floral sofa, steering clear of the coffee table and the rows of occupied shoes. Naturalizers with saggy nylons: Martha. Hush Puppies with argyles: Gramps. Tidy beige pumps: Martha's daughter? Italian loafers with translucent black-ribbed socks: Martha's son-in-law? Assorted unisex sneakered feet, and, way at the back, before the doorway through to the kitchen, a very old, thick-ankled pair of feet in orthopaedic shoes. I don't look up. If this is Grandma, I don't want to know.

I look away from this forest of ankles and chrome chair legs only to find my eyes settling on family photos. A young man in a naval uniform. A teenage girl in a purple grad formal, clutching a long-stemmed rose. A beaky groom, standing, his arm around a bride, seated and smiling demonically, as in don't-look-now-but-I've-just-sat-on-the-potato-salad.

And then there is the oval-framed photo portrait of a grey-haired couple. Martha's folks? They look smooth and clean, pension more than adequate, infirmity not set in yet. I have to keep reminding myself, "You are here," like the little x on a mall map.

Gramps is now stiff-necked and handkerchief-to-brow while I get down to the Stones' "Can't You Hear Me Knockin'" sax solo. The son-in-law eyes me like I'm a neat little unit he'd like to test drive. Martha smiles glassily at a fixed point in the fire. Spittle has formed in one corner of Gramps' mouth. Who is this man, in his hunter's shirt and corduroys? Did he grow up around here, shooting ducks on what is now this paved subdivision with streets named Eider and Teal?

I lie on my back, reach over my head and grab fistfuls of dacron wool in my vampirella talons ("Passion Pink," by Maybelline), and writhe like I'm just about to orgasm, turning my head from side to side so some hair catches in my mouth, rubbing one foot against the inside of my other ankle. Delicately, not wanting to seem coarse. From under half-closed lids I look at each of the men by turn as I slowly move my hands from my ribs up under my breasts. I am kneeling now, neck arched back so my hair hangs down to the rug. Then arch, kick, up, pose (perspiring, seeing the purple prom dress, the groom's beak, the Geritol couple), and it's almost over.

I canter up to Gramps. My vulva is a foot away from his hand. He could reach out with a sugar lump, as if it were a pony. I bend, my butt in the son-in-law's face. Behind him, his wife (?) gasps, having spent the last twelve minutes fooling with her necklace. I bus Gramps on the cheek.

"Merry Christmas." (Huskily.) Exit, stage left. Martha, now lurking in the hallway, stuffs some bills into the pocket of my robe as if I were an unwanted trick-or-treater.

"The cab's on its way." She ushers me into the restroom. She's surprisingly strong. I wash with one leg on the tiled counter, a jug of dried flowers and a china kitten with cottonballs for brains next to my foot. Also, a twin frame in which I recognize The Beaked One and The Graduate. As I reach for the stack of fluffy peach towels, Martha's hand thrusts a small, fraying object through the door.

"Here's a towel for you," she sings. I can still feel the force of her hand on my lower back. Good thing I didn't

134

skid and break my leg on the shiny hallway lino. They'd probably take me out behind the barn and shoot me.

Haven't seen Lloyd in almost a year. Thought I'd have saved money by now, but I just bought my first sequinned costume, six DJ-made tapes, and my shoes need replacing after ten work weeks (three hundred to three hundred and sixty shows).

I'm lucky I'm getting steady work, now that more straight girls are walking in off the street willing to strip (having heard how it's such great money. Wait till they find out how much it costs). And that's not all that's changed since Meg got edged out by the male agents. Plastic surgery is upping the ante, tan lines and Vegas-style costumes are *de rigueur*, also routines are more gymnastic. Whenever I take a week off I tell myself I'm going to make a plan to get out, get off the circuit, then I just sleep until it's Monday and time to go on-stage again.

Monday, January 15
Prince Rupert

"If you can give a children's puppet show," Meg used to say, "you've got what it takes to strip." Down to stockings, I lean against the gilt-veined mirror, my head back, my wrists over my head together as if chained, and move my rib cage in a slow figure eight. This is a restful move, the end of a mellow night in this bar full of fishermen. Most of them are out on the water, but there's still fifty guys here, each of whom has a freezer full of sockeye somewhere, individually frozen in blocks of ice.

I scan the rows of men: old and grey-bearded; young and narrow-shouldered; honest-eyed, wistful-eyed, unconsciously agape. Self-satisfied, bored, hopeful, nonchalantly searching, confused. Men in Greenpeace T-shirts, black muscle shirts, white T-shirts printed with the names of brewing companies, buttondown workshirts, the young bucks by the pool tables in mesh tanks.

Seeing the child in the man. That guy with the greasy blond cowlick stretching his seriously built bicep down the green felt, lining up a shot. He was a child once. Rode a little plastic truck around the fenced yard of a subdivision. Drank Kool-Aid. Got chickenpox. Threw up in a movie theatre. That enormously tall Native guy in the heavy metal T-shirt, the one with his feet up on one of the front tables, looking at me, looking at his beer, looking back at me, trying for eye contact. He was a child, too. Whined for more pie. Threw snowballs at passing cars. Shot a rabbit and cried over it. Learned to knit from his grandmother.

Then there's me. What if I were just wearing cotton underpants, no makeup? But I can't bear to think about it. I've worked so hard for this and here I am, the queen of all your gazes.

Vancouver General Hospital. Twelve years old. The night before the first operation. Seeing myself from above, floating, still intact, hair fanned out around me, framed in the oval tub. Saying goodbye.

I knew I would never be the same.

"I don't usually go to these places."

"So what are you doing here?"

"Lars, there. He's my boss. We do drywall." The kid waved me over to sit with him. Might as well please management. Besides, the only book I have with me is about pre-Christian matriarchal culture and it's just too weird to switch from women being revered to crawling around naked on all fours in front of a roomful of men.

"Oh, yeah? That's cool." The kid has large pores and eyebrows that meet in the middle behind his spectacles. His stringy hair is in a ponytail. A radical, I think, hope rising. Maybe even an intellectual. They're certainly thin on the ground in these parts.

"Can I ask you something?" He leans forward and his eyes glint strangely. "What are you *really* doing here?"

"Making money." And then, for some reason, I lie, "I'm an English major. Third year. I'm taking a year off to work. I'm saving for a computer." He splutters his beer. You'd think I was a talking horse.

"Can I ask you something personal?" he says. "Do you ever feel *in conflict* about your role?"

"In conflict?"

"You know. Guilty."

"Oh, gosh," I laugh. I feel comfortable with this kid. I have him down for a sociology student.

"I think about this a lot. I mean, how could I not? I've read Steinem's essays, the ones about pornography and Linda Lovelace, you know? I hate to think I'm letting down the cause but I'm kind of stuck. I mean, since I don't have a degree or a trade or folks with money I can either flip burgers for minimum wage or cross the Madonna/Whore line and make some good money. Like Margo St. James says, 'A blow job is better than no job.'" The way he is looking at me I add, "Not that I'm a hooker, of course." Then I feel guilty for saying it. What if I *were?* The same reasoning would apply.

"Why are you telling me this stuff? I didn't ask for this."

"Pardon me," I say haughtily. "I thought you did."

It is a good night for stripping. As my last song starts, I lower myself slowly to the floor in a graceful split, my scarlet fake fingernails fooling with the gold elastic of my G. I press my chest into the rug and spin my legs around, then kick them up, bringing them down slowly in a pin-wheel backbend, courtesy of Starfire, who showed me this on the floor of her room at the Cariboo Inn in Williams Lake one morning before breakfast. The lights are warm on my belly. The rhinestone chain drips from my waist. The black light picks up the twelve-inch fringe of the cupless bra; beneath it, I am certain, the scar is invisible. I can feel the tension of the men—can almost feel them breathe—below the smoky jazz trumpet. As I put on my robe afterwards, a surveying crew (baseball caps, day-glo vests) draw their chairs in closer.

"Great show."

"Great costume."

"Sort of Western."

"Yeah. Spaghetti Western."

"Why, thank ya, darlin'." I am Miss Kitty this week. "You'll all stay for Bridget, won't you? She's on in fifteen minutes. And I'm on again at one." All the time I can feel Ponytail's gaze across the room. He is staring, eyes popping, from my nipples to my feather garter to my face. I give him my girl-next-door smile and he scratches his head.

"What about you?" I say, sliding in beside him while the other dancer is on-stage. "What are your plans?"

"Huh?" He can barely take his eyes off B's pussy but when he does his gaze is accusing. "I'm taking a year off, too. Normally, I attend Fraser Valley Bible College. I major in the word of God." Around 1:30, as I emerge from the shower, it hits me. He didn't mean *that* kind of conflict—he meant, did I feel guilty for being such a sinful creature? I throw back my head, towelling my hair vigorously, and laugh and laugh.

Bridget, a chubby blonde from the Fraser Valley who's stripping so she can buy a horse, does a baby doll show in which she wears a diaper and plays with balloons.

"At the end of my show I sit on one. It makes a loud pop. The men love it." I wouldn't have thought that would be erotic, but then men are getting weirder every day. Last week during my floor show a guy nudged his neighbor and said, "She wants to be spanked." He smiled at me. "Don't you?" I guess that was a reasonable interpretation of my body language—I mean, I *was* lying on my tummy wriggling my bottom up and down in time to the music. The whole thing gets so automatic. Then there are the guys who sit right up front and lay a hand, palm down, on the stage. They want you to step on it during your first or second song, when you are strutting around making whipping gestures and looking mean. They always look so pleased and surprised when you come over and pretend to grind your spike right through their hand.

She was chatting with the manager in his tiny, fluorescent-lit office under the eaves when I arrived. She was leaning forward, her robe open to the waist. Her mane was wild and scraggly, the colours of mustard and ragweed. Her voice stopped when I entered. Her puffy face turned towards me.

"You're the Lioness Linda," I said. "I've heard of you."

"Of course you have. Everybody has." That voice. Deep and raw, as if her throat had rusted. "I had such a good time I stayed. Isn't that right, Rob?" She laughed. "So you're in one of the upstairs rooms tonight. But you can visit me."

The elevator's broken so I wrestle my luggage up three flights of stairs. The numbers on my room key tag have worn away. The corridor smells like wet raincoats. Bare bulbs pick out the strange stains on the wallpaper, throw shadowy shapes where it is peeling.

My room is painted surgeon green. It contains a bed, a table, three misshapen hangers, a bare light bulb with a string pull, no mirror, no phone, no electrical outlets. So much for the reading lamp I always pack. The bathroom is down the hall. Not a soul is around, it seems. I sit on the edge of the bed. I do not remove my coat or boots, only partly because it's so cold. The curtains are still; the window is closed. Brushing them aside with caution—I can't shake the sense there's someone here I don't want to surprise—I find the room looks out on an alley, across which a fire escape mars the face of an apartment building. Some of its windows are cracked. Those that aren't in shadow reflect a neon calf, thigh, the curve of hips, improbable breasts, or part of the words EXOTIC ENTERTAINMENT, from the giant Valley Motor Inn sign above me. What a great shot this would make for a photographer from *True Detective*, especially with me in costume in the foreground, sprawled in a pool of blood. It is this last thought, and the sudden urgent desire for company, that propels me to the doorway of the Lioness Linda's room.

It's a nice room. It's got ankle-deep pearl grey carpeting and powder blue walls and a big makeup mirror framed in Hollywood lights. It takes me a full minute to notice there's someone in the king-size gel bed. Sleeping. She's so still. A girl of about fourteen, fair and exquisite, partially draped in the fluid lines of the sheet. Like a figure carved from Ivory soap. Her hands are folded under her cheek.

"My sister," says the Lioness, lumbering towards me. Involuntarily, I shrink back. "I said to my mom, 'Whaddaya mean, dumping that brat on me?' But I'm stuck with her. What a fucking pain." There's something almost, but not quite, reassuring about the Lioness, solidly packed into black leather pants and a black T-shirt, a couple of studded belts creatively accentuating her crotch. Her hair is a lank switch.

"Come on in here while I pack." Her movement releases a smell: cigarettes, something sweet, underneath it something sour. She folds turkey feather boas, cat costumes, polka-dotted hoop skirts, and stows them away in three big black trunks. She holds up a red-hooded cloak.

"You know this? 'Hey There Little Red Riding Hood?'"

"Sure," I say. "Sam the Sham and the Pharoahs. I do it too."

"Sure, honey. Everyone does it." She laughs her raunchy laugh. "Only when I do it I put my skirt over some guy's head—grab his head and bring it to my crotch. People sure laugh at the look on his face when I finally let him go. I'm thinking of doing a Bo Peep show if I can just get hold of a sheep."

"What about management?" I say. "Most places won't allow animals. I heard Carmelita's having trouble getting booked since the white rats her snake eats kept escaping on her last road trip. Starfire says the chambermaid from the Trapline in Fort Nelson hasn't recovered yet."

"Oh," the Lioness looked scornful. "I don't take any shit from *management*. You see, honey, I'm a name. I'm often busted for lewdness, and I'm held over a lot, too. I'm a big draw. And I don't take no shit. I throw desks, chairs, whatever I feel like—right out the window. Three storeys. Hell, once I even threw a bed. That was from five storeys. Management was really dickin' me around that day. Plus I had a hangover." That laugh. "How old are you, honey?"

"Twenty" I lie.

"Ooh, just a baby." I wince and say nothing.

"When I first started eight years ago I was eighteen. Pure and blond. Shit, I even had short hair. That was at the Venus Theatre in Guam. The other women were real rough, putting things up themselves. All the time I was on-stage the manager stood in the wings, going ..." She makes a spread-your-legs gesture with her hands. Her eyes are pale green, rimmed with blue pencil. I look into them for the first time and think I see corpses, clouds of flies.

She finishes folding and plops down in the director's chair in front of the makeup mirror. I follow her back to my spot near the door. After a moment it opens and an auburn-haired woman brushes past me to the mirror.

"This is Shasta," says the Lioness, from somewhere far away as Shasta sheds her robe. What a give-away look of envy, of longing, must cross my face, taking in the beauty of her perfect tanned body, pointed breasts, that smooth, uncut abdomen. Shasta shoots me a look— brief, sharp, closed—from Florentine seraphic eyes. Then she tosses her hair and climbs onto the Lioness' lap, puts her face close. Their figures, one clad in black, the other bare, reflected in the mirror. Their hair, blond and rust. I murmur something about "leaving you two alone" and withdraw. As I shut the door behind me the little sister stirs in her sleep.

As I'm crossing the lobby after the L.L. interlude, a guy (slightly built, wispy moustache) comes up to me.

"Hey, aren't you Tabitha?"

"Who are you?"

"Don't you remember me? I've seen you dance."

"Oh?" I'm confused.

"Sure you remember me. You looked right at me." From a lot of stages, footlights can make it seem like you're looking deep into their eyes when you're only seeing red-veined darkness. "Want to do some coke? I have some great stuff back at my place. Fresh off the plane. I got connections."

It is on the tip of my tongue to say I never do unidentified substances with total strangers. And then I think of the Lioness, her enviable way of taking up space. I think of all the other strippers I've met, who regularly drink and snort and smoke and drop and shoot and are still walking, still hanging out in bars across B.C., their high-heeled feet propped on the chair next to them, draining the liquid from around their ice cubes as they laugh and tell stories. Intact, having apparently lost nothing, but having gained a huskiness of voice and a savagery of gesture I would like to have. *Shit*, says a little voice in my head. *You are such a snotty, precious little prude.*

"It's just through here," he says. One-thirty and I'm walking beside him, leaving behind the brightly lit hotel, turning down another alley and another one. Stepping across a puddle with the sky shining off it, criss-crossed telephone wires scarring the surface. Skirting trash cans. ("Young lady," said Dr. Klein the day after the first operation. "We've saved your life." *For what?* I thought. I still wonder.)

"It's just up here." I follow him up four rotting wooden steps to a door in the back of a warehouse. In the tiny kitchen encrusted dishes are piled beside a hotplate. Nearby, an empty tin of beans. Its sharp-edged top gleamed nastily, a septic instrument.

"How many lines would you like?" he calls from the other room. "I'm just chopping it now. Jesus, this stuff's rocky." I move to the doorway. At the opposite end of the narrow room, he sits on the edge of a cot, doing something on a plywood plank across a plastic milk crate. On the cot is a bare mattress, a withered pillow, and a torn army blanket. There is no other furniture in the room. But it is the walls that cause me to stiffen like a sleepwalker waking on a subway track. The walls are the bright, unnatural yellow of drug-laced urine. They are covered in black Magic Marker. There are drawings of male and female genitals, a dripping head (sex unspecific), "fuk."

"On second thought," I say carefully, "I've changed my mind. But thank you anyway." I smile politely, with effort. Seventh grader from Little Flower Academy meets Manson's biggest fan.

"You're sure?" he says, adding, "I'll do your share then." Quickly, as if I might change my mind. He is talkative on the way back. I stomp briskly, planning to gouge his throat if he grabs me. But he only wants to talk—urgently, with a grating hoarseness. I glance at him; he's trying to make eye contact. Sweat streams into his strangely alight eyes.

"You remind me so much of my ex-girlfriend. You know her? Baby Buns. Come on. You must know her. Long, straight brown hair? Like yours. Nice ass. That's why they called her—"

"What happened?" My voice comes out low, calming.

"She left me." His voice breaks on "left." He gulps. "For another woman. Another stripper. She took the baby, too. Tabitha." He touches my arm. I jerk it away. In high school the visiting woman cop showed us how you could let the guy kiss you—even kiss him back—*then* knee him in the groin. No way I'm letting him kiss me, I'm thinking, and then the hotel heaves into view. Never have I been so glad to see a ten-foot-high neon naked woman.

6 a.m.

Quite the charming night it's been.

Got back to find the door doesn't lock. Tried to undress and found I couldn't. I felt someone watching me but of course I was alone. I switched out the light and

147

lay on the bed fully clothed. But I couldn't close my eyes. I kept feeling whoever it was hovering by my bed. So I jumped up and switched on the light. Then lay down again but of course couldn't sleep with the light. The green walls didn't help.

Around about five I gave up and am now sitting in the lobby beside the night desk clerk, Norman Snead (no kidding). The rest of the staff, all straight from an Alfred Hitchcock movie, have long gone to bed. Norman is sixteen with skin you could blot with a paper towel, the way you drain bacon. He has been enlightening me about his *Penthouse* collection, on and on in his nasal drone.

("Miss January, now. She's a brunette. Says her name's Tammy and she likes bowling. I consider that quite a coincidence, see, because my birthday's in January and you know what? I love to bowl.") Thank God he's gone to get us some coffee from the 7-11 which is somewhere out there. Through the long flat window over the lobby doors the sky is beginning to lighten. From where I sit the clouds look curdled. My mouth tastes sour. My handwriting lonely little letters, hunched and strung out like starlings on a telephone wire. Probably unreadable later. Oh, good—here comes Norman with the coffee.

The room I shared with my sisters was down the hall from Mom and Dad's. Every night, when they started yelling, I'd crawl in with Elspeth, and Rona or Elspeth would start.

"Life Savers, salt water taffy, molasses kisses ..."

"Tootsie Rolls, chocolate-covered peanuts, butter-scotches ..."

"Licorice allsorts. What else? Sour cherry drops, chewy mints ..." Or we'd play A my name is Allison, my husband's name is Albert. We live in Albequerque and we sell angel food cake. But when our older brother and sister moved out, Rona and Elspeth moved upstairs to take over their bedroom. I was four and just beginning to run to the bathroom a lot (no blood yet), so I stayed in our old room, alone. I didn't know what they were yelling about. I only knew that the whole house crackled with my mother's frustration, her stomach muscles clamped down on her voice so that it escaped through her gritted teeth compressed, like a note written on very correct stationery and slipped under a door, that says, *I would like to kill you.* The open-throated yell was my father's.

I wanted to make them stop, but I never dared their closed bedroom door. Once, though, in the afternoon, when they were fighting in the living room, I crept down the dark, green woven hall carpet—a long, long way— with the idea that I might try to stop them. I wanted them to be like they sometimes were on Sunday, my mother making coffee and my father taking me to Max's deli at Forty-first and Oak for lox and poppy seed bagels.

But when I got to the end of the hall, I froze in the doorway. My mother, snarling the way I felt when I ground down hard on my guts, slowly picked up the brass bowl from the coffee table and raised it to her right shoulder as if to strike him with it. As I watched, breathing shallowly, she slowly, tremblingly, put it back down.

I played with spoons under the dining-room table, building a barrier of rhythmic noise against the tornado of fury in the kitchen, my mother alone in there, talking aloud. "For me, nothing should go right. Everything should go wrong ..." Always, this sentence the centrepiece of her monologue, accompanied by a rising, whinnying whine like a possessed vacuum cleaner preparing to levitate and fly out the window. Her key would stick in the Valiant's old lock, a pan would scorch or a slice of toast stick in the toaster. (*Oh no.* I would cramp up in the next room, put down my spoons or big wooden beads or plastic zoo animals, jam my fists up under my ribs and rock, also mad at the peas, at the toaster, at the *bad* molasses jar that had plummeted from her hand— "wouldn't you know it?"—and spitefully splashed its sticky dark brownness all over the linoleum. *Bad! Bad, bad, bad, bad, bad.* Could I have prevented it? I wondered.) And she'd be off, wrapping herself around and around in a haze of white-blistered furious despair. She often ended up rocking back and forth on her knees, face covered in hands, a spit-forming litany of bashed and dented pieces of words escaping through the cracks between her fingers.

Sometimes, when she'd gone to lie down for a nap, ("Do *not* disturb me") I went through the cupboards and screwed on lids, tight enough so that the jar wouldn't slip from them, but not tight enough to cause trouble.

After they divorced, Dad took to pounding on the door. Bam! Bam! Bam!

"I demand to see my children!"

"Jack." My mother, wearily. "Go home. You're frightening the children." Over the next four years, though, a pattern developed. We would hear his tread, slow and heavy, on the front or back stairs.

"Oh, no! It's Dad!" Mom would whisk into her room like a rabbit down its hole, pull her blinds and shut the door, first announcing in her low, clenched voice,

"I am not available." Dad would be broken up in the three diamond-shaped panes of the front door, his face all screwed up in a gut-twisting mixture of loveable hurt feelings and adult scariness.

"Rona? Elspeth? Sarah! Come on, kitty. It's your father. Open the door."

"We can't." Elspeth, wide-eyed, rhythmically squeezing her hands.

"Why not?!"

"You know. Mom says there's a court order." But some-times I would end up in his white Toyota Corolla, en route to his one bedroom apartment, him sighing heavily beside me, as if I had done, or was doing, something wrong.

"Sit here and don't make any noise." When we got there, he would spend the rest of the evening playing chess with Farrell Newcome, a fellow English professor. They drank coffee and quoted things to each other.

"My cat Geoffrey ..." Geoffrey would let me pat him but he wouldn't be picked up. Farrell was missing one thumb past its knuckle. Once when Dad went to make more coffee, Farrell turned to me and slowly worked the stub of his thumb in and out of my mouth. It seemed a very odd thing to do.

"Do you like this?"

I looked at him, puzzled, then looked away. He laughed softly. That was in March—they'd been quoting over the early daffodils in the vase on Dad's desk. At lilac time, one day when we were alone in his kitchen, I told him what Farrell had done. I wanted him to know; I wasn't sure just why.

"Farrell did something really weird," I began. As I con-tinued, Dad's body seemed tenser and he got red in the face.

"What are you saying about Farrell?" he demanded.

"Nothing. I don't know. I felt funny when he ... I always tried not to look at it so he wouldn't feel bad like there was something wrong with him, but did he have to put it in my mouth? And was it rude of me that I didn't like it?"

"Stop. Just stop right now. I don't want to hear any more about it."

The back door frosted glass made him an enormous silhouette. I did not want to go with him. I did not want to be where I was, either, pressed flat on my stomach under my bunk bed.

I didn't want to be anywhere.

Thursday, February 22
White Rock

Sitting up in bed at the Ocean Beach Hotel. Ginger is onstage doing the 4:00; it's dark out. Poor Ginger. She slept with the bar manager, and now he won't talk to her. I bet the full-length mirror is a one-way window. I can't stand in front of it without imagining the work crew that's next door fixing up the honeymoon suite gathered around it, rating me. This job is really fucking me up.

Yesterday I did my pale-blue baby doll set twice—the

one that ends with "Love Slave," where I wriggle around and pretend to scratch myself, act like I'm coming. I can see myself in a mirrored pillar. There's a place in the music where I'm kneeling with my head down and to one side, hands together behind my back, tied with a chiffon scarf. So I did it twice and fell asleep late, long after the 1:40. Both times it went great.

"Hey baby," a cute sturdy-looking blond guy in tight Levis said to me. "That was out of this world. Real erection material." In real life you'd slap the guy's face. I think. I can't remember.

I said, "Thank you, my dear," in my best Tempest Storm manner. Got back to my room and smoked a joint with Ginger. She went off on the bartender's hog (cherry red flames painted on the gas tank and ultra-long front forks. A real chopper. Pretty thing. Too bad there isn't some way you can ditch the guy and fuck the bike. I must be tired), and I wandered around this big pink dressing room, scuffing my feet in the long white shag, sipping at the roach, singing softly to myself—"Walking After Midnight."

Management here loves strippers. The curtains are pink. The bedspread is pink. The dressing table ruffle and its plush stool are pink. In the bathroom, the big old cast-iron tub is pink. On the walls (pink) are framed promo shots of someone named "Missy." She's sprawled on a motheaten bearskin rug in front of a mottled backdrop. She has a tattoo on her forearm. The photographer must have majored in forensics. He's done a beautiful job of the bruises up and down her legs. She's either clumsy or athletic or both.

Woke up just now from the following dream: I'm onstage, kneeling, in my blue baby dolls. I reach up and my rhinestone bracelet gets caught near my mouth. I turn away from the audience, let them look at my rear end, play with my panties with my left hand while I try and figure out what my right wrist is stuck on. Turns out it's stuck on my scarf and ... the scarf is coming out of my mouth. I sit up so I'm kneeling again and tug harder. The scarf is tied to another scarf, which is tied to more and more scarves, knotted together, coming out of my mouth in a wet, dark line. I turn to the audience, which I can normally see from this stage, but it has gone dark. All I see are my wide, horrified eyes, reflected in the pillar mirror, and below them the rest of me, entangled and thrashing.

Wednesday, February 28
Duncan

My room overlooks the back roof. I am afraid of being broken in on, raped, stabbed, etc. I would ask for a different room but for my don't-make-waves policy. Lioness Linda I'm not. These days, what with my dark hair and small breasts, I'm just trying to hold the line: show up for my shows on time, be polite to audience and management, keep a low profile. I'm not making top money any more, but it's still better than any other job I could get.

Woke around 4 a.m. from a grainy newsreel dream in which a voice-over declared that, "Escort services are the number one form of female suicide." In otherwise empty streets, workmen, using hooked poles of the type store owners use to fetch down a dress displayed near the ceiling, or being lifted up in cherry-pickers such as linemen use, were removing clear plastic garment bags containing dismembered pretty women from the bare trees and telephone wires. A typical bag contained a perfect body (big breasts, no cellulite) with the painted head beside it. Or a torso with head still on it but limbs all arrayed beside.

The camera cut to a dumpster which was full of these bags and some corpses not in bags. A high-heeled leg stuck over the side at a grotesque angle, like that stewardess in *People* years ago, whose pilot husband murdered her by stuffing her in the deep-freeze. (I read about it at the hairdresser's yesterday, where I went to dither for the umpteenth time about going platinum with waist-length weaves. Ended up chickening out as usual and got a sort of purply rinse, mostly to make Wanda, the new graduate from the local hairdressing school, feel better.) Then the camera began to pan in on a lone head. The mouth was open wide. The eyes were a clear, baby, supermodel blue.

I woke up struggling to fill my lungs. Between the pub door and the door to the lobby, which I have to stop and unlock on my return from the stage, is a fluorescent-lit, grey-painted cement corridor. It doesn't help that the bathroom mirror makes me look more the scarred geek than ever.

Early a.m., Saturday, March 2
Drizzling rain.
I'm in bed; thirty shows down, six to go.

I think I hope that one morning I'll wake up to find my abdomen as smooth and uninterrupted as the hundreds of tummies I have seen by now, in all shades, with or without tan lines, a few with rings or jewels in the navel. Baring themselves insouciantly, innocent of having been vandalized, their owners having never given two consecutive minutes thought to the security of their organs.

When a naked woman walks up to a three-way mirror—on-stage, or in a dressing room—I see her organs in triplicate sleeping behind her skin, which is at once as transparent to me as the cellophane across a Barbie doll box, and as indifferent as hard plastic.

Four weeks ago, in the mall in Kamloops, I bought a Vacation Barbie. I've slept with her under my pillow every night since then. Just now I operated, little plastic shavings on the *Playboy*, open to Kimberly, whom Barbie resembles in miniature. Only now both of their careers are finished, I'm afraid: K. has suffered a disfiguring slash, and I had to pull a nail out of the wall, displacing a small oval picture

157

of a black-and-white kitten in a basket of poppies, in order to make the hole in the lower right quadrant of Barbie's abdomen. I wrapped her in one-inch flesh-tone micropore tape—which I just happen to have on hand—in order to stanch her Cutex blood.

Last night. Glen, one of the owners, walks me across the parking lot to the bus depot. It has rained. Litter from the Kentucky Fried Chicken stand (breasts, thighs, and wings in boxes) lie all around, sodden.

"Nice of you to do this," I say, since he's carrying my luggage.

"That's okay," he says. "You're a pretty good girl. You're welcome to come back anytime." We sit down on the bench outside the closed depot. There is one other person waiting, a pallid, willowy young man.

"Excuse me," he says. "I couldn't help overhearing. I'm the DJ at the Pink Pussycat in Victoria." The two men talk shop for a while. The DJ only talks to Glen. Finally Glen addresses a remark to me.

"So. You liked it here?"

"Oh, yes," I say. "The crowd was nice. DJs were nice." Why do I always go past it? When someone is the least bit nice to me I start spilling my guts. "The hardest part about stripping is at night sometimes." I add, like an idiot, "You never know when Death might be shimmying up the drainpipe in a stocking mask."

"Oh," sneers the DJ. "A poet." He sits behind me on the bus. Bars of milky light pass over his face, his long straight hair, as the bus moves up-island in the dark, past Ladysmith to Nanaimo.

"I never thought I'd date a stripper," he's saying dreamily. "But she's a perfect 10. Paradise."

"What's her name?"

"I told you—Paradise." He's suddenly irritable.

"Oh, sorry." Why do I apologize to this pallid, sulky youth who will go on and on about himself, never inquiring about me? But I do. I even ask him questions to draw him out when it seems like he might be winding down.

"She's vegetarian ... That's right. Just nuts and seeds." (Laughs.) "Oh yeah, and a lot of what do you call them? Bean sprouts. We plan to live on a houseboat. We're both water signs. Oh, yeah. A lot in common. We're both into Jim Morrison."

"What's work like?"

"Oh, yeah, it's okay. We get some pretty kooky peelers, though. Last month one hanged herself in her room." I am fully awake now.

"Why?" I say carefully.

"Oh, you know. She had a fight with management. They were going to fire her anyway," he adds, as if that explains everything.

"Why?"

"Drugs. Her mind was shit."

"But," I say slowly. "Just a sec. She may have been taking

159

drugs because she was depressed. Not suicidal because she was on drugs. Drugs just amplify the way you're feeling. Shouldn't the question be, 'Why was she originally depressed?'"

"She was fucked up," he says sharply. "She didn't know what she was doing."

Monday, Revelstoke

Can't stop wondering about the woman who hanged herself at the Pink Pussycat. Did she leave behind an address book with more numbers crossed out than current? A son or a daughter in a foster home? A collection of hotel matchbooks, like mine, from all the places she's danced?

I find I want to know—urgently—what she hanged herself with. I picture a harem-girl costume, with jewelled cuffs and underpieces and a gold-sequinned belt coiled like a live thing. It is the first thing she lifts from her battered suitcase in the shadowy room with the cracked walls and canned music about wanting to make it with you, baby, coming up through the creaky floorboards, and the hiss of indifferent strangers, neatly boxed, speeding away down the Island Highway. A hot, overcast day, little bits of white paper fluttering among the blur of cars. She stands there in the dim, shabby gloom. The scaled thing across her wrists glitters: *use me, use me.*

The two young men and their girlfriends have come to the bar for a lark. The girls hang back at first, but then they toss their blow-dried heads and follow their guys defiantly right up front, where they all sit back, look up at me expectantly as I do what I think of as my "Fuck You" set for the 8 o'clock show. After a couple of songs I look down from the brass pole, on which I am holding myself with one leg, trying not to show exertion on my face and delicately pulling on my nipples so they'll stick out more, and notice that the young men are hunched forward. Each has one or both hands around his face.

The two girls are still sitting back. The brunette's head is turned. She can't take her eyes off her boyfriend. She touches his knee. He puts his hand on her thigh but doesn't look away from me. She sees that I have seen, blushes and flees for the washroom, leaving her beer behind, untouched.

The blonde views me stonily, as if she were a young male doctor from a hundred years ago, about to cure me of unseemly sexual appetite. She looks like she could be a med student. I whirl, feeling the cool, disturbed air streak by my lower ribs, the sweat flying off my nose. Moving (slow, sleek hip rolls with a shoulder undulation, sliding slowly down the pole in a barber-shop swirl, then dropping to the floor in a swan split), I try to abort these thoughts before they form.

Afterwards, she collars me as I am pausing on the stage steps to check if both cups from my removable-cup bra are folded up inside my burgundy plush rug. If one of those yahoos steals just one cup, there goes the bra and therefore the whole costume while I scramble to find a replacement—or make one, sitting up in my room between shows with scissors, pincushion, a yard of twelve-inch fringe (which doesn't come cheap), and a package of rhinestones (ditto). We strippers are a wild bunch.

"Can I ask you something?"

"What?" I say, backing away slightly.

"Don't you feel you're being exploited?" I sigh, take off my shoes and stand flat foot, looking up at her, eyeing the pens clipped to her pocket. I am aware of my bare collar-bones above the sweat-soaked peach satin of my shortie robe. (It's polyester. I wanted silk. But I was lucky to get this for $10.99 in a bargain basement.)

The sturdy neck of the college girl asserts itself above her crisp button-down oxford shirt. I imagine her striding along the aisles of the upscale department store down the street. Her underwear drawer would contain matched sets of top-of-the-line yummies sprinkled with rosebuds. She'd choose cotton, not being starved for lace. Docksiders would idle on the polished hardwood floor beside her bed, waiting to be got into like the boat down at the summer cottage.

Sometimes, on arriving in a new hotel room, I walk around and marvel. Cute little bars of soap. Stacks of fluffy towels. Glasses wrapped in paper. New sheets on the bed. All for me. Somebody vacuumed—for *me*.

"No," I say. "I don't see it. I figure I'm the exploiter. I mean, look at these guys." I gesture and she looks around, catches sight of the brunette's boyfriend downing a shooter and staring at my ankle bracelet. "I'm exploiting the fact that they think with their balls."

She crosses her arms. "I don't buy it," she says in a loud, clear voice. "I mean, how can you choose to participate in this system?"

I yell, "Because I'm fucked up!" then run from the room.

I curl up on the hotel bath mat until it is time to climb into my red and black dominatrix set for the 10 o'clock show. I spent a lot of time curled up on bathroom floors a long time ago. I've started again.

"Why don't you get up?" They stood on the seats of the toilet stalls on either side, looking down at me.

"Go on," said one.

"What's that?"

"It's blood."

"Eeew. She's shitting blood."

"What's wrong with you? You're shitting blood."

"Go on, stupid. Tell us."

"She's not talking."

"She's too stupid."

"I'm sick," I mumbled.

"She's si-ick."

"Ugly, too."

"Who would you like to be queen of the class?" asked Miss Morrow. All the boys' heads swivelled to Jacquie; all the girls' heads followed. She bowed her honey-coloured head and looked at her hands. Finally she got to her feet, making a face, kind of rolling her eyes as if to say, "Oh, all right. If you insist."

"How does she do it?," I thought, sucking the blood from a hangnail. "What's her secret?" Simone, behind Jacquie's back, gave the teacher a sweet smile, then turned her ice-blue eyes on me and sneered knowingly.

(Aesthetically, Simone was a tiny perfect pre-adolescent Vacation Barbie, except her long, wavy blond hair was not knotted to her scalp like a doll's. Rather, each strand sprang pristine from its own tiny pink follicle. You could see this in action if you stood behind her, say, at the pencil sharpener, before she "accidentally" jabbed you, smiled and glided off. Like Jacquie's and Leanne's, Simone's tan was perpetual. It came from real sun, shining on some part of the world known only to Simone's parents, who whisked her off there regularly.)

The boys' presence was vaguer but somehow pervasive. They ignored me except to deliver a note from a girl, or to throw me a rotten orange. ("Catch!") It seemed to me that they took their cues from the girls, but I wasn't at all sure about this. Over and over, I saw their heads swivelling on their necks toward Jacquie, like sunflowers obeying the sun, or the tide being dragged by the moon.

While I dutifully formed barbed rows of f's and seas of pointy-topped s's (like seals with their noses in the air), worked at long division, and tried to build a bridge out of modelling clay and drinking straws, my mind was elsewhere.

Mid-afternoon
Thursday, March 7
The Revelstoke Motor Inn

"How did you get the scar?"

I tossed my hair, said, "Knife fight," and took off.

"Looks like you lost."

I made a face and called back, "You should've seen her!" They eat this shit up. It's what they want to believe, and I guess it's okay. I'm drawing a crowd, and the men keep going on about me.

("Gorgeous. I can't believe how gorgeous she is."

"The perfect body. Un-fucking-real.")

I never get tired of it. Pure, cool glacier water in my mouth, only I'm not allowed to swallow.

At least I get to be alone a lot. I'm lying on top of the sheets. It's a big, corner room with a high ceiling. Oval plates in the diner downstairs. They built this town a hundred years ago, for the railroad. Surveyors, engineers, firemen, loggers and millworkers stayed here. They must've wakened nights as I do, and lain here listening to the wailing train before it chugged around the bend, over the narrow steel bridge spanning the Columbia River canyon and off into the pines.

The Canadian Pacific Railroad was new then. The town was full of men, and a few enterprising women. There are mobile homes and vinyl-sided subdivisions now, but the downtown's still got that wild-west look, those old wood buildings with the false fronts. A few women made a lot of money off these same dumb guys, just the same dumb guys who never finished high school but who get to own the subdivision house with the four by four in the semi-detached garage, and who get all that just because they're men. (Where's *my* high-paid union job?) I walk around the town and wonder if those women were lonely in their rooms, if they ever felt connected and at the centre of the action, or if they figured that life was elsewhere and they were stuck slowly aging where no one could meet their eyes and really see them.

I like to just lie still and think like this. Little scraps of sunlight high on the wall, reflected through the glass of water by my bed. My feather boa draped along the oval mirror tilted in its stand; the dressing table covered with all my little pots and brushes. I run my hands over these narrow hips, feel my small, hard thighs. I look in the mirror and am reassured. Plausible. I look the part. I just keep running my fingertips over my chin and throat and the silky undersides of my breasts. Mapping out the territory. I am real and I am still here. I am here, safe behind this locked door, and I am pretty sure I am real.

Wednesday, March 13
Peninsula Motor Inn
Gibsons

It snowed this morning. I'm eating yesterday's cold fried chicken. This Inn is the damnedest place—miles out of town and no food but hot dogs. I'm here to replace Rexella, who leaves tonight. The other dancers are Suzy and Sex Toy.

5 p.m. Friday, March 15

Got a ride into town this a.m. with old Don of the dead, bar regular and part-time handyman here at "The Pen," who told me how he made two hundred thousand dollars prospecting one year.

"But I drank it all up," he chuckled, then lapsed into a long cough while slowing down for elk, the gear shift all but coming off in his hand. "Had a great big party and drank it all up." He told me about Rexella, the stripper I'm replacing. ("Now, there's a girl ain't gonna live long.") He said she arrived with pneumonia and a couple of cracked ribs, then fell down some stairs at a house party and landed on her wrist.

"I brought her home at the start of the week and Abby, that's the head chambermaid, put her to bed. Next morning she was standing out front the motel, on the edge of the highway, just wearing a thin shirt and boots. We came up behind her, real slow like, and whispered, 'Rexie? Hey. You still workin' for us?' She turned her head then, slow, and you should've seen her eyes. Well Abby just picked her up and carried her back to bed. We brought her a cup of tea, said, 'You know, we were just kiddin'. You don't have to dance. Look atcha. Your ribs're taped. Your wrist is in a sling. You wanna go home?' But she said—she could hardly talk, you know? She looked at us. She said, 'I have to dance. I need the money.'"

"She did her shows?"

The trees-followed-by-more-trees landscape dissolved and was suddenly replaced by the word Bargains! in pink neon script above a startling jumble of green corrugated tin and Gothic arches. The mall.

"Ay, she did. Couldn't use the poles, mind you, or roll around too hard, and you could see ..." He looks down and coughs. "You could see she was hurtin'." He rolled a cigarette, and his smoke met my breath in the cold air. "She left the other night with two fellas, about twenty-one,

and all that was left of her paycheque. Guess how much."
His face, above his blackened hand, was an old, sad
hound's, eyes rheumy and red-cornered.

"A hundred bucks?"

"Twenty-five." He put the words down quietly. "No
home anywhere, turns out. Just drifting on the road."

We sat in his old blue Maverick and stared at the
Pharmasave across the parking lot as snowflakes slowly
obscured the lines between reserved and handicapped and
I wondered if everyone is in pain with their life, only in
some it's a sliver embedded in a translucent palm and in
some it's the heart banging deathlessly on its hinge, like a
bird that's been hit by a car and wants to be hit again.

Just after the 5:45

Cripple wagging his stump. (At the beaver bar, a.k.a.
gynecology row, looking up at me as I wait for the music
to start.) Calls out, "It's hard, baby!" Thump, thump. "It's
hard for *you*." I go to flash him my showgirl smile but turn
away and do not look again at his laughing, knowing eyes.

Friday, almost midnight

"Those are nice. Are they real?"

"What, my tits? Of course not. My mommy bought

them for me." Suzy smiles at me in the mirror. She stands barefoot in a red, white and blue sequinned T-bar ("The sailors love this one." They're up from Seattle and are throwing money on the stage like Americans always do), putting on makeup. "She bought us each a set for Christmas. But see," she moves aside her waist-length black hair, "The surgeon made them too small. He said he thought I was a nice girl and he didn't want men staring at me. I should've gone to someone else. I waited years for these."

"The men must love 'em."

"Who? The pigs downstairs? I didn't get 'em for *them*. I got them for myself. I wish they were bigger but at least they turned out. Last week I was at the Alder Inn with Dorielle when one of her implants came loose. Was it ugly. Corner of the bag poked right out the side of her breast. But she had a kid at home, like I do, so she needed the money. You should've seen her, covering her tit all the way through. Pitiful." But I am familiar with the casual hand covering some Chernobyl of the self-concept, some Bhopal of the body.

("Aw, c'mon. Let's see," call the blond, ball-capped construction workers. Dorielle smiling like those kids on telethons, who've lost something they always wanted, almost had, and know they will never, ever get over having missed.)

"I made her show the manager. 'He'll pay you,' I said. 'You can't keep doing this through fifteen more shows. It won't work anyhow. They'll catch on.' The bar was almost empty when she opened her robe and showed him. He looked scared, started checking around to see if anyone else saw. Said, 'You gotta get out of here. Right now. You can't dance like that. Sure, I'll pay you.' He did, too."

"So what happened?"

"Heaven Leigh flew in from Fort Liard that night, to replace her. And you know about Lalique, right? Stripped for Teasers Two, out of Edmonton? *Her* implants hardened like concrete. Had to have 'em sawed off. She's home now. Flat as a board. Gets headaches and has a rash. She'll never work again and she's all fucked up about it."

"What happened to Dorielle?"

"Oh. Her. I don't know." She slips on a red bustier, a navy jacket with gold braid, and a white, vaguely nautical hat. Turns to me and shrugs. "Just another fucked-up chick."

The backdrop to my life on the B.C. strip circuit is a continuous belt of fir, cedar, pine and elk, rolling by as if cranked by some tireless member of the actors' union. The songs go on and on and I am trapped under the hot lights smiling and bending from the waist the way they like still letting down my hair the way they like but I'm sad the way they all look the same and when I do my floorshows now, behind the face that is smiling at them and pouting and cutting my eyes and playing with the

T-bar the way they like (pulling it between my legs as I take it off, squeezing it between my thighs and pulling it with one hand while stroking it with circled fingers), they don't watch the hockey game, no, they don't play pool, and even with the encores, behind this wind-up, scented, glittery self, I'm lonely anyway.

I'm in the back seat of Mr. and Mrs. Management's dog-hair-lined Oldsmobile. Sex Toy OD'd last night.

"Young people today don't know how good they've got it. Right, Marion?" snorts Ed. We pass a trailer park with pots of petunias out front and a hand-carved wooden sign, "Drifters' Rest." Closer to the water a woman lugs a heavy-looking baby outside The Good Earth, a health-food store. The baby is waving a wet lollipop around. As I watch, it comes to rest in Mama's hair. Ed's voice unravels like a scratchy wool sweater as we pass private-school girls arguing vigorously over a soccer ball.

"Why, in those days people queued all day at soup kitchens. Lived on molasses, pretty near." Blah, blah, blah. Sex Toy, when drunk, had a distinctive Native accent. (Suzy: "I asked her once if she was Indian but she wouldn't admit it.") Her hair a scrambled nest of peroxide.

The abandoned dining room and kitchen lay between our rooms and the bar. Passing through one day and seeing the vinyl chairs upended on dusty tablecloths, I'd stopped and imagined the diners who once came and ate off their knife points and swilled hooch from the bottle and belched and grabbed the legs of a younger Marion.

"I've been a waitress all my—. Been in public service all my—. Worked in the hospitality industry all my life," I heard Marion tell Rexella when I arrived. "Now, you've got to *smile*."

"Yes, ma'am," said Rexella, and swayed off with her own crooked, dreamy little smile, on the arm of a pleased-looking sailor. But I kept hearing how Marion corrected herself twice. Guess she didn't like the sound of, "I've been a waitress all my life." Who would? Through the kitchen window, across the rain-soaked grass, something bright moved beneath a willow tree, before a path leading into a bramble thicket.

Finch? my first thought. Then, garbage? Some bright candy-wrapper? (Behind me, in the ghost café, the meat slicer hulked, its steel screens and circular blades a spent cock, an unloaded gun. Chalked-up specials from the days of the boys-will-be-boys diner: beef dip, soup, fries. Beside me, plink, plink, plink. The roof leaking into the zinc sink.)

No. Not garbage. Sex Toy, in her psychedelic cowboy pants and fringed jacket, twirling at the edge of the empty lot in an old tire swing. She was sprawled in it, dangling weeds from one hand, throat thrown open to the sky. I went up to my room then, and drew my face with HB pencil, looking in the cracked mirror over the dresser. (Lipstick kisses on the wall beside it. Different mouths, in two rows. The dancer's room. I pressed my lips to the cold paint, coral beside magenta.) I drew the crack in the mirror, nice and dark, jagging through my left eye.

I should have waded out there, holding out a cup of black coffee, or a hot dog.

I have been fantasizing as we drive, leafless alders veining the surface of the peninsula, silver as a compact spilled from a purse in daylight, of leaning forward and strangling the pair of them with one of my fishnet stockings, the way a wanted hitchhiker will do with his belt.

"Nervous, Marion?" Ed murmurs, and I learn she is going in for a cataract operation. We are at the ferry terminal now, the gangplank being lowered on chains.

"Yes, I'm a little nervous," I hear her say. "Silly, I know, after all these years." He tightens his arm across her cardiganed shoulder and she leans into him. It's not their fault that I'm so maladjusted. It's not their fault Sex Toy went out last night, already shitfaced on whiskey, and took eight unidentified pills from a guy she'd never seen.

She made it up the stairs after he'd dumped her off at the front door, and then lost it for good in the corridor outside our rooms. Suzy found her collapsed, eyes open, focussing and clouding, and then clouding more than focussing, cracked voice calling for someone (Marjean? Margie?). Bare under the white vinyl jacket, nipples like a woman who'd given birth. Worst of all, the joes and mikes and daves leaning in their doorways up and down the hall, beer cans in hands, watching Suzy's nails digging into the little armpits, dragging her, me trying to pull her zebra pants back up over her thighs. Sour smell, shreds of Aqua Velva and the little gold clit ring gleaming. The joes eye it like a dime they might want to pick up.

"She was a good girl," says Mrs. Management as we disembark. "She waited until the end to have her shebang." (Is that what it was?) "She didn't miss a show." It starts to rain. That downturned smile, those bitten hands carving something into the bar with her room key when the bartender's back was turned.

We pass an auto yard where a man in overalls bangs repeatedly on a car's private parts. The hood is up, and it stands impassively while his forearm slam slam slams, his features scrunched to the centre of his face. Bang that sucker home. Mr. Management almost rear ends a police car, he is so busy watching. As we pass the cop car, the cop's head turns to follow my lips, painted "Siren Red."

"You're saving up your money, aren't you, dear?" says Mrs. Management suddenly.

"Yes, ma'am." I still think about going to college, but this seems less and less likely. With every passing show I get more afraid of straight people.

"Here's what I think you should do. Save up until you have enough, then buy your own free-standing concession. You buy a loaf of bread, see? Costs you maybe two dollars. And a head of iceberg lettuce. And one of them industrial-size jars of mayonnaise." I consider this as the small coach of her conversation lurches forward. "Do you know how many sandwiches you can make with that one loaf of bread?" She is looking at me brightly, nodding. "And you know what you pay for a sandwich when you go to a coffee shop. And if you can make soup! People used to come from miles around for my clam chowder. You could make a tidy profit, I know you could."

"Yes, ma'am. Thank you. I'll keep that in mind." We are heading up Twelfth Avenue, passing Vancouver General Hospital. The same stretch of road I've been flying down, blank-eyed and bare-assed, in my dreams since I was five years old.

Monday, March 25
Golden

Can't stop thinking about this guy I met Saturday at Courtenay House on Vancouver Island. It was Ladies' Night when our shows were done. We were going to kick back and watch the male dancers when it was over—watch *them* sweat, for a change. Jason and Nino had already arrived with their whips and Madam, Nino's boa constrictor. Jason kept vying with Steffi Staxx for space in the Hollywood-lit dressing-table mirror.

"Move those tits of yours before I get the milking machine." Steffi shot him a disgusted look—"Fuck off,

Jason"—and went back to her hair, scrunching about half a can of mousse into it. She goes through more mousse in a week than any dancer I've seen. Her hair seems to require it for its whipped confectionery texture.

Sasha arrived in his toreador pants, French inhaling. So overdone. Then CeeJay showed up, rounding out the line-up, and with him this gorgeous hunk. I opened the door while tying my cat-ears on under my chin and there he was, greeting me in that half-smiling, sardonic way that keeps making me think of Rhett Butler. His eyes were the colour of sultanas.

"Uh, who are you?" I said stupidly.

"Vance." Still looking directly at me, he pointed past me at CeeJay, who was limbering up against the radiator, having already stripped to a loincloth. "I'm with him."

Steffi whipped through her show, skipping the first song which cut it to ten minutes, which is a no-no except on a full-house night like this with screaming women lined up three deep on the sidewalk. Management is either lenient or oblivious. They were running us all back-to-back so I followed her, trying not to feel inferior. But I cleaned up in tips, since there was a table of drunk Americans right up front. One of them threw a loony at me. It hit me in the lower back and now I have the perfect imprint of a loon in my T-bar zone, surrounded by an edge of blackening bruise.

When I got back to the room Nino was already coming out of the can with his thing tied off and waggling in front of him—you could tell—under his black vinyl G. I didn't stare. Neither did Steffi, but the four men did. Nino made a show of covering himself with his girlie book, which only made them howl. Then he grabbed his snake and climbed through the trapdoor, down the brass ladder to the stage.

Steffi and I, crouched in the sound-and-light booth, didn't much get off on the shows.

"It looks so stupid, doesn't it?" she whispered to me when CeeJay was finishing up, having oiled himself all over and strutted with dry ice in the background, courtesy of Vance, who sat above me in the booth, exuding—I could swear—heterosexual warmth. He smelled like cinnamon, cloves, and lemons. He reached down and rubbed my shoulders after he'd set the lights for CeeJay's floor-show so that now, as CeeJay humped his rug under shifting shades of rose and coral, while the bouncers held the women back, I could feel Vance's hands digging into my shoulder blades, working at where I wrenched my right shoulder trying to copy one of Steffi's moves.

"Are you gay?" I got a chance to ask him later, whispering in his ear over the shrieks of the women, their long applause. Still looking at CeeJay, he did that "*comme ci, comme ça*" thing with his hand.

"About seventy-thirty, I guess. I like boyish women." That rules me out. Still, when I told him I was going to be in Vancouver he said, "I'll be house-sitting. You can stay with me."

Steffi is sitting at the dressing room's makeup mirror, putting on pink lipstick from a tube striped like a barber's pole. Her hair is mostly wheat blond, maybe peroxided (but maybe not—she seems to have been born beautiful), curling just below her shoulders.

But it is her body, her body I focus on. Barely covered by a hot pink spandex top, a matching mini, leaving bare most of her long legs, (brown from long sessions in the tan-bed), her serenely scarless tummy. Her clothing doesn't do much to hide her big new fake-but-who-cares tits. Breasts. Boobs. Hooters. The nipples show through the fabric, which hugs their curves and the curves of her buttocks, so tight, so damned high and small and tight. She totters around in her stripper spikes, looking gloriously stupid, at once higher and lower quality, trashier and more exotic, than your ordinary, garden-variety woman.

"Bend over," I think. "Bend over." She walks across the dressing room and bends from the waist, pouting out her soft little puffy lips for "Pink Taffi Swirl." Her nails are short short, an exciting hint of the girl next door.

I watch her on-stage. She's twenty, a cheerleader whose mom sent her to gymnastics classes. I can't describe what she can do with her body on those two brass poles on-stage.

But at one point she simply leans against one of them and pulls her top up. Slowly. Those moments when her breasts bobble free, you can feel the room grow rigid, the collective sucking-in of breath. If it weren't for the taped music playing inanely on, I assure you, you could hear a swizzle stick snap.

Back in the dressing room:

"Are those real?" I ask.

"No, of course not."

"Who did you go to?"

"Warren. In Vancouver. But," she adds. "Look here. See how they're sort of puckered across the top?"

"Uh huh." I nod politely.

"No. *Look.*" I move forward a few paces to look more closely at her opulent cleavage. I see a faint, shiny pucker across the top of each breast. Once I sat at the knee-treadle sewing machine at the kitchen table of my mother's house and tried to trim a school skirt with satin ribbon. I remember how the ribbon puckered; I was frustrated at not getting it to lie smooth.

"See?" She whispers, sounding concerned. "Here. Feel." Tentatively, I draw my finger lightly across the furrow. Part of me is with her, concerned; we have both been worked over by doctors. The other part of me can't believe my good fortune. She's so silky my fingertips only get the general idea. She even feels like satin ribbon.

"I see what you mean," I say carefully. "At least it's not noticeable. Will it go away?"

"He filled them too full," she says. Her eyes are baby blue. "I went to see him, and he said they were perfect, no problem. He told me to roll them, like this."

She puts a hand on each and rolls them, first out away from each other, then up, over and down toward each other. I feel myself separate again: one of me is sympathizing and hoping it works; the other is photographing her for my jerk-off picture file. I am sickened at myself. This is outrageous—botched plastic surgery that could give this young woman cancer, liver damage, God knows what else.

So much for my belief in the personhood of young women. I know she's a complex human being with what should be an inalienable right to fulfill all aspects of her potential. I also know I will call her a bimbo later in those wordless movies that play behind my eyes. I shouldn't be like this. I should send my movies to the feminist film launderette and have them returned to me with the patriarchal-oppression-perpetuating content edited out. (Won't be much left.) I should ... I can't "should."

The summer after the second operation, I stayed up late at night in my bedroom, running my index finger up and down my freshly-reopened-and-stapled-shut scar and turning the pages of a particular *Vogue* that featured a blond TV actress whose hair style was everywhere, and whose tummy was seen, expansively bared, between the pieces of a micro-bikini, every Thursday night on TV. The article contained black-and-white photos of her as a child, water-skiing and playing badminton, as well as polaroids from her debut as Prom Queen, and, one of my favourites, her leaning against the door of a sorority house, smiling offhandedly down at a group of muscular young men, who gaze adoringly up at her. Lastly, a lavish, coloured pictorial of her at home. There she is, leaping, tennis racquet poised, short, pleated skirt a white butterfly, the famous mane floating around her face like a golden appeldoorn tulip. There she is again, by her swimming pool, in a mini top over bikini bottoms (tummy peeping) and again, this time inside, wearing a cardigan, reading a novel on a couch in a high-ceilinged room with a fountain—*yes, indoors!*—in the background.

The humidity glued the sheets to my legs as I flipped back to her childhood Christmas photos (angelic figure in white nightgown cuddled between loving parents) and forward to a shot of her bedroom (where they pointed out her satin sheets and sliding door onto sand and palm trees), always returning to the sorority shot. A grasshopper chirped in the front-yard elm. My fingertip read the Braille staple sites, from number 1, inches below my left breast, through twenty more, down into the long gold hairs that were beginning to darken.

I fantasized:

"Who's there?!" She sits up in alarm, clutching the satin sheet to her peignoir, the famous hair fetchingly tousled. A figure emerges from the drapes, billowing in the breeze off Malibu. She gasps, then sighs, smiling, and shakes her head. "Why, it's a girl. Come closer. Tell me, what is your name?" I end up kneeling on the many layers of throw rugs on the deep carpet beside her bed, cuddling in her tanned arms, which gleam with some opalescent lotion, while she murmurs soothing things and rakes her famous square-manicured nails through my hair.

Wednesday, March 27

Golden

The Golden Nugget Pub is tiny. The stage is about a foot high, four-by-six feet, no pole, no mirror, no nothing. The kind of thing some guys set up in the rec room for a friend's stag.

This morning, keeping Holy Tara company while she dresses for the 11:00. It's a fourteen-hour shift here so we've got plenty of time between shows. Not long enough to go anywhere, just enough to sit around. We each have our own room, and there's a makeshift dressing room down the hall. I sit on top of the mirrored makeup bench that runs the length of one wall and hug my knees, watching Holy, who's wandering around in a fuschia sequinned bra and G-string, smoking a cigarette.

"Where were you last week?" I ask.

"Whitehorse. Shit but it's cold up there. Damned near

froze my butt off walking to the Mohawk for smokes. How about you?"

"Penticton. Just did the Okanagan so I'm doing the Kootenay circuit."

"You got an old man?" She pauses to snap a sequinned T-bar over the G-string and wiggle into a tight dress of the same fabric. She wears long false nails, has platinum blond hair, a slight potbelly, and a couple of tattoos—a butterfly and a rose.

"No."

She looks at me almost curiously. "Live alone, then? One of those fancy West End apartments?"

"No. Uh, I have a room in a shared house." This is almost true. I mean, I will when I go down to stay with Vance in Vancouver. For some reason I'm too embarrassed to tell her I'm living on the road, no boyfriend, no fixed address. As if I'm too much of a failure to have a social life.

"Now, where'd I put that whip?" She finds it on top of the TV. "Great." Draws on thigh-high patent leather spike-heeled boots. "Well, I got one. *Had* one, I mean. We're like ..."

"On again, off again?"

She gives a short, hoarse laugh. "Yeah. Right now we're off. He's runnin' around with Silky Sins—you know her? But I got him back. I like to have a good time, you know what I mean?" Her eyes narrow as she leans against the radiator, head tilted back, exhaling through her nostrils.

"Met some guys in Fort St. John. One of them was cute. Real nice—had this great big stallion on his back." She fingers the rose on her collarbone. "I packed with him up to a quarry one night, me and this other chick with him and his buddy on their hogs. Built a fire, drank some tequila." She's sitting beside me at the mirror putting on false eyelashes. Holding one eye closed, she turns to me. "Hope I'm not pregnant."

"Didn't you use anything?"

"Hell no. I don't even know if we did it."

I think, I'm nineteen, and I'm going to have to go on living and living and living. She chops some coke on the back of her *Playgirl*. "Myself, since I do oil shows, I feel like I live in the shower, trying to get the baby oil out of my hair. Want some?"

Remembering Christmas at the Capri, I say, "No. Thanks."

"You serious?"

"Um, yeah."

"Not a narc, are ya?"

"No. I ..."

"Gave it up, eh? Smart you. I spent eight grand in a blizzard at Christmas." She laughs. "Oh, well. All the more for me, then." She unwraps a paper packet of soda straws and sucks it up, then goes back to dressing, now bustling around. "Hey, did you see that blond over by the pool table? On the left, from stage. He's wearing a 'Motorhead Rules' T-shirt. I'm going to try for him." I look at myself in the mirror. I look tired. I haven't been with a man in so long I've almost forgotten what it's like.

Six in the morning and still dark when the bus pulls over to the side of the road and I see a sign saying Bow River. All night we have been passing mountains topped with glow-in-the-dark snow. I'd been on the bus about half an hour—we'd just passed a sign saying "Ottertail 35 km"—when a hand reached between my seat and the window and poked me.

"Psst. Want to smoke a joint?"

"How'd you know …?"

"I can always tell a dancer."

Krystal is crunched in next to me, leaning against the tiny metal sink, holding onto the handrail, me on the toilet, ditto, as the bus winds through the virgin forest of Banff National Park. Even in the dark, I know the water sloshing two feet below me is a deep, impossible blue.

I think she might be the Krystal who's rumoured to steal, so I keep my Lancôme lip wand (bought because a certain model in *Vogue* who I think I might bear a slight resemblance to used it to good effect in a fashion spread set in St. Tropez in the January issue) out of sight when I dig through my purse for matches.

"Where'd you just come from?"

"Revelstoke."

"I just did there, before Golden. Come to think of it, I think I heard of you in Golden. Krystal Wild?"

"That's me."

"Well, they're still talking about you in Golden." A slow smile lights the powdered face, behind the long, black hair. "Are you the one who got the guy in the face with the—?"

"—dildo full of shaving cream. Yup. Shoulda been there. This old, broken-down pig was in there every night yellin', 'Hey! Get the fuckin' squaw bitch outta this town and let's see some *real* pussy!' So one night—Thursday, I think it was—"

"You put up with that shit through, like, eighteen shows?!"

"Yeah, well. I got friends who would've been happy to arrange for his dental surgery, but I didn't have the heart. So I says, 'Psst. Big boy. Yeah, baby. I like 'em big, like you.'" As she winks, sliding lights from the empty highway slip over her open eye, her closed lid, just for a moment. "'I'll give you some real pussy,' I says. 'C'mere.' So he does. 'Closer,' I says. He does and all of a sudden I squeeze, real fast, and—"

"Splat!" We say together. Pass the joint back and forth in silence.

"I wish I had your nerve," I say quietly, after a while. I want to reach out and trace my fake fingernail around the

187

edges of the fat marijuana leaf on the back of her fake-fingernailed hand, but I don't know her well enough. Its outline looks tattooed on but it is filled in with green felt pen. "Where before Revelstoke?"

"Kamloops. Williams Lake. Quesnel."

"What's Quesnel like?"

"Injun town. Loggers. But lots of injuns. Bet you hate Indian towns." She looks at me slyly. "All you whities do."

"Yeah," I say, stupidly.

"It's easier when you know the people. Like Smithers. I got cousins, eh? Take me out, hot days. To the narrows. I gaff with the men. Cliff's edge. Catch salmon with a long pole's got a hook on the end. Very sharp."

"Wow," I say. "Sounds hard."

"Big thing is, just don't lose your balance." She laughs. "It's a long way down, and it's fast water. Lotsa rocks."

"Do you see eagles?"

"Oh, yeah. Bears, too. They're out after the huckleberries that grow all along those bluffs."

"I love huckleberries."

"Me, too."

Outside Calgary by several hours still. At Morley Flats the scenery changes. The steep forests edged in yellow bell lilies and white flowering dogwood, the sharp switchbacks over deep, treed ravines of the British Columbia interior end suddenly and are replaced by flat fields. I don't know where I'm going. The agent said Alberta's where it's happening, and he just got a bunch of new gigs there.

Ever since Meg's out I've had one agent after another. I'm doing like everyone else now and have a whole bunch of numbers in my telephone book. Strewn through my luggage are little cards printed with the silhouettes of naked women, like you see on truckers' mudguards. Several times a day I ponder the diagram I saw of implant surgery: the breast being cut away from the bone and lifted up in order for the gel bag, with or without a coating of furniture-upholstery foam, to be slid underneath, like a gourmet recipe for chicken breasts, deboned and stuffed. I think of the parts of the woman not shown in the diagram, all of her, splayed out on the operating table under those bright lamps like on an airport runway. I get agitated, start pulling the skin away from my thumb cuticles. Sometimes I look down and my hands are a bleeding, sticky, slippery mess and I don't know how it happened, and I scold myself the men will see. They see everything. Everybody sees everything.

Where has Al decided to send me? What if I have to walk three blocks to get to the stage? What if I have to share a room? Hard to say which worries me more—having my costumes stolen or my notebook read. (Besides which, how can I hide my weird need to write? I'd have to write in the bathroom, late at night. Oh, well. Wouldn't be the first time.) And of course what if the manager lets himself into my room and rapes me, like Krystal said happened to Missy Scott in Lethbridge?

"Aren't *you* going to Lethbridge?" I said.

"You bet." She was bending forward, stowing her Nike bag under my seat, and she paused and looked at me through the slit between the seats. Krystal stared at me, and I stared back, and I thought she was going to say something and changed her mind and then she must have changed it again.

"What would it matter if he did rape me, anyway?"

"It would matter," I said, and reached around. We held hands for a couple of miles, there in the belly of the predawn Greyhound, not moving when a baby started to wail or even when a gangly man in a cowboy hat got up to go to the john. His penis passed us at mouth level but we didn't care. Our eyes had found each other's again, and held, and dropped, and sought and held again.

Now I stare at the sun, a huge red disc rising—just across a field or way at the edge of the world, I can't tell—and try to burn down to just me, here, with Krystal sacked out behind me (I must've been sleeping, too), just enough money on me for fried eggs and ketchup and hash browns, or whatever, somewhere.

We pass abandoned wooden shacks, bright yellow fields of canola punctuated by the odd redtail hawk on a fencepost, keeping an eye on the fields the way 7-11 clerks watch the video monitor when Native kids head for the candy aisle. "Alberta Wheat Pool" block-lettered on the side of a tall, painted brick building, the twin steel silos gleaming red in the blaze from the horizon. In the seats ahead of me, the fat, kerchiefed women are beginning to grunt and feel around among the many string-tied cloth bundles and plastic bags around their feet. We pass some wooden sidewalks, then a general store straight out of a movie about cheerful, porcelain-skinned whores with perfect dental work and musical inclinations. Next to it is a neon orange plastic video store postered with guns and (sigh) more tits, this time fairly leaping from a white bikini, the woman's face, above them, in shadow.

Bus depot washroom, Calgary

They didn't stop to let us eat, so I'm queasy and crashing. My scalp itches, my hair feels stringy and I've shed a couple of my GlamourElle nails. Resolutely not looking in the mirror.

Graffiti in here some kind of record low—lots of hearts, as in, "I (heart) Travis," another little heart dotting the 'i' in Travis. Travis just wants your tight little ass, sweetheart.

I didn't see Krystal when I got off the bus. But, feeling around in my purse for a pen just now, I found a fat joint with a happy face drawn on one end.

"Welcome to Hooter's." A pair of stuffed, pink felt breasts crowd the visor of the DJ's ballcap. "We have some promotional extras we expect you to participate in—your agent probably told you. Tonight is Best Bikini night. Tuesdays—Best Buns. Wednesdays—Best Gymnastics. That's where you can really show off your polework. Thursdays—" Even if I didn't care about getting a rep with the agents as difficult, by Monday afternoon the booking game is locked. From the Ocean Beach in White Rock to the French Maid in Calgary to the Trapline in Fort Nelson, girls are shaking out their G-strings and steaming out their costumes in the shower and doing leglifts on the floor of their rooms.

"Got that?" I must seem stunned, because the DJ snaps his fingers in front of my face, passes his hand back and forth, windshield-wiper-style, as if I were not all there. Am I all here? I think I am going to cry. With neither a garter belt nor a removeable-cup corselette, and under those bright lights, there is no way I can go through a Best Bikini contest. It is out of the question.

The DJ booth is papered in promos, mostly of bands with one syllable names—Rod, Slur, and, obscurely, Bake. They all look the same to me. It's not just the bands. It's something I'm noticing about men in general.

Snakeskin boots or business suits, preppie or biker, on parole or wearing a Rolex, I'm having trouble telling them apart.

Amber Lynn in wet-look vinyl chaps poses with her butt to the camera. She also has gorgeous long, curly hair. And those *tits*. But Pandora Peaks' and Honey Mellons' dominate the booth. Ms. Peaks' are pasted on the glass at eye level with the DJ, so that when on-stage we are framed beside them in his view. Plastic surgeons, here I come. Ms. Mellons' are just behind the DJ's head, so that he appears pillowed against them. I don't know how long I can keep this up. I doubt that now I'd even get hired at Burger King.

Later, same day

My handwriting like baled-up barbed wire, black and tangly. Pressing so hard I'm coming through the paper in places, and that feels so good I want to slash store mannequins and stuff the gashes with tangled up red videotape, red fibreglass insulation (hah!), or red-dyed cheese curls and stuff a half-empty bag of beer nuts in their stupid mouths. I see that I'm not quite right but this notebook is mine. I bought it. Nobody will ever read it but me. I can say whatever I want. It's still a free fucking *cuntry*. Yeah, and I'm the beaver on the nickel. It's not the fault of any of these good citizens around me that I'm fucked up. It's not Al's or the DJ's or Honey fucking Mellons' fault that every time I walk through a lingerie department, aisle after aisle of unmolested tummies taunting me from the bra boxes ("We're normal. We're normal. We're normal. We're healthy. We're sexy. Buy me, buy me, buy me"), it's like ricocheting through a hall of mirrors. Who's fault is it? How come if I write long enough I always come around again to this?

Sitting on the bathroom floor of the North Centre Inn, Centre Street North, Calgary. Room 202. Black and white hexagonal tiles. Tub rust-stained where the cold tap leaks, a small, insistent runniness, like the nose of the kid you meet in any supermarket, in any city, whining about his allergies. The windows are painted closed but rattle when trucks go by. Kitten Kane, the dancer I'm sharing with, hasn't showed up yet. I need a toke. Face it. I'm freaked about tonight. There's no way I can pull off a bikini contest. I need a plan. (Across the street a man and woman are yelling at each other in front of a bin of sneakers outside a place called Bargain World.)

"May I speak to Wayne, please?" I'm calling from the lobby, paved in gold-flecked lino. The number inside the matchbook (Tumbleweed Motel, Cache Creek) is faded. The matches are soft, a row of impotent magicians' pinkies.

"Pardon me?" She sounds too perky to be a bike chick.

"Wayne." My voice comes out a low croak. I recite the number.

"That's the number here, but I'm afraid you've reached Look To The Son Christian Daycare."

2:15 p.m. Tuesday

"He was a good bartender—an excellent bartender. I never had to worry about my stock. 'Never safer than with a Lutheran,' he used to joke. But after his wife left him for a Jewish accountant we never could trust him again. He was still an excellent bartender—never forgot a face, gave advice like Dear Abby, never smelled liquor on his breath. That was the strange part. I think he drank leftovers. No, he'd finish his shift, clean up, and just as he left the building—Wham! Flat on his face, cold. I'd've kept him on, but I was afraid one day he'd get it together and sue."

Arnold Samson, Owner, as it says on the brass plaque next to a refillable plastic pint coffee mug, was on the phone when I knocked and wiggled in, wearing my tight grey leather mini, seamed stockings and lace top with push-up cups. He smiled and waved at me. I smiled back and slipped behind him, massaging his shoulders and scritching my hands around his bald spot. I thought the next part might be awkward, but he just said,

"Hey, what are you ...? Mmm. *Mmm*," and "Say, listen.

195

Can I call you back?" into the phone, then settled back and closed his eyes.

Here I am, back in Room 202. Small, sparse raindrops blow at our window, clean streaks showing up the dirt. Beyond the tops of semis and an ice-cream man shaking his fist at a taxi driver, a slight, dark-skinned figure leans against the wall of Bargain World. Man or woman, I can't tell, but I feel the echo move through my body—arms hugging self, head down, rocking. I'm heading out now for another tiny notebook and a bottle of mouthwash.

3 a.m. Thursday

Twenty-four down; twelve to go and I'm a whore now, but at least I have a roof over my head. Turned my head away when I met Arnold on the stairs yesterday a.m. He went from how-ya-doin', glad-ta-see-ya overjoyed to skulking off, head down, looking confused. That makes two of us.

Anyway, no doubt he'll give me a good report on the Agents' Report Sheet. ("Rate the dancer between I and 5 on the following points: Breasts, Muscle Tone, Dance Ability, Costumes, Music, Polework, Public relations, Punctuality, Overall Bar Patron Satisfaction." Too bad there isn't a spot for fellatio.) I didn't even make any money. God only knows what Shalimar would say. Hah.

Is the Heavenly Host here, presiding over Hooter's?

Can't sleep. I remember how Shayla (Vixxen) used to come off-stage practically spitting teeth, she was so mad. "I hate them! They yell, 'Hey squaw. Hey Pocahontas. And I was wearing my *schoolteacher* getup. I don't *do* a buckskin number. On and on about my tits. Fucking creeps. Bastards. I hate them." I remember how we tried new styles on each other's hair and ate beef jerky and sugar cookies and tried to teach ourselves moves from the music video station, and one time—it was late—she leaned across the night table to where I lay in my twin bed and whispered, "Hey. Tabitha. Who do you wish you were?" I named my blond actress and she named hers and we fell asleep and woke to trucks clambering up the exit ramp in the sizzling rain like so many slippery mud turtles. I remember she wore "Hawaiian Ginger" and had the magazine ad of the beautiful Polynesian woman taped inside the lid of her makeup box and we promised to write but we both keep moving around, and I ask after her but she must've changed her name again. I hope she's okay. I really hope she's okay.

Middle of the night,
Saturday, April 6
(Twenty-five down; five to go.)

Kitten Kane's been gone the last three nights, sleeping with the drummer from a band called The Rod and Gun Club. But now she's back and lies on her bed smoking hash-oil cigs. I lie on my bed, and we stare at the stain on the ceiling, which is shaped like a kangaroo.

"How old are you?"

"Nineteen."

"Uh, Kitten? I turned nineteen on-stage in Kitimat last year. Reckoned it was my two thousandth show. How old are you really?"

"Sixteen." God am I tired.

Sunday, on the Greyhound

Haven't slept in more than forty-eight hours.

What is respect?

The busdriver treats me with the deference due all good girls. I must look like one today. But when Kitten steps up beside me and I tell him, "We're going to Edmonton," his manner changes. He grabs my ticket roughly. His eyes tear up and down my clothing, stopping briefly to look coldly at my face. Respect is what you're given in exchange for reassuring people that they are healthy, that nothing has gone wrong.

Kitten went out and partied last night with Barbie Dahl and Serena. I stayed "home" and read *Harper's*, wondering if those cultured, witty, gentle-sounding men are different from barscum, or if they rate you for fuckability just the same. My eyes feel like prairie sand has got up under their lids.

Kitten Kane got off in Edmonton.

Four hours out, the Greyhound climbing north, I start thinking about how not many people live in this part of the world. 8 o'clock, no home lights breaking the thin dark of fields: I think of owls out there, skimming the cold grey air, scanning the grass for fieldmice.

A Native woman nurses her baby under a shawl across the aisle from me, at the edge of the reading light's dim golden circle, beneath which a guy my age, asleep over his guitar case, clutches a *Time* magazine open to the page where a rock star blew his brains out. The guitarist looks cramped in his seat, his head against a bundled up, blue ski jacket. Knees curled around the neck of the guitar case, knobby wristbones pale under the dark hairs. Homemade, partially-inked-in tattoo of a lion, studded black leather vest. In the back of the bus, his band mates are sprawled in a nest of comic books and orange peels.

"I come from Faust," a voice behind me is whispering. "That's near Driftpile, on the Lesser Slave Lake." The bus climbs higher and higher on the map.

I feel like an astronaut who has been cut loose in orbit and has been drifting around in space for years.

Monday, April 8
Fort St. John

Coffee shop. Staring at my bowl of bean soup. Drinking questionable water. (Some say that it will make me sick, others that it only tastes foul.)

The other dancer, Deanna Jones, is twenty and has been dancing two years. She's dating a drummer in a country band. ("Every band member I've ever dated has been a drummer.")

5:30 p.m. Tuesday

Staggered through five shows last night. Just got through my good ol' naughty schoolgirl set—kind of lame but I did it. Sitting on a mound of fishnets and garter belts all tangled up and fighting with each other. Whoops and whistles from downstairs as Deanna does her flaming-torches-cartwheeling cheerleader set. Just hunted fifteen minutes for my makeup bag before finding it in the bottom of my duffel. Christ, I'm exhausted.

Still haven't slept. Must be some kind of record.

An hour later

I just quit. I don't care. So tired I can hardly see. Two minutes to showtime and the zipper on my green spangled skirt broke. I gave away six shows. Enough money left from Calgary to get to Vancouver (five hundred and twenty miles), where I'm booked through a different agent, but not much left for food.

5:45 a.m. Wednesday, April 10
Fort St. John bus depot

Deanna's been trying to get pregnant by Daryl since they started dating, six months ago.

"All I want to do is be a housewife. Stay home, raise my children, and keep my man happy so he won't look for sex somewhere else. My mother was always working, never at home for me, and I suffered because of it. I'm gonna be there for my children."

That was her longest speech. It emerged about two in the morning, after her last show. The phone rang when she was on-stage for her 10 o'clock. I answered it.

"Is Deanna there?"

"No. Is this Daryl?"

"Yeah."

"She's on-stage right now, Daryl, but if you leave your number I'll get her to call you right back."

"Thanks, uh, that's okay. I'll call back." Deanna sparkled when I told her he'd called. Christ, she's beautiful, tall and long-limbed, silky and perfumed, with that long dark brown hair, those pretty green eyes, that voice: low, hesitant, raspy.

Next to Deanna's sequin costumes ("In B.C. you can get away with anything for a costume. In Alberta you have to have sequins, so I'm buying only sequins") my green spangled skirt and white-fringed cowgirl outfit look pathetic. In fact, most of my costumes look pathetic next to hers. In fact, *I* look pathetic next to her. Her skin has a freshpicked apricot glow. (Do I look like that? I shouldn't get into this on so little sleep. Of course I feel like dog food.) She looks like a movie star in her champagne-pink sequinned gown.

I watch her do up the front-closing bra over her C-cup breasts. The little valley between them gleams pale against her tan.

"You have a lot of costumes?" I ask.

"Five or six. I'm trying to get more theme shows. I've

got a nine hundred dollar California Raisin costume on order from this lady in Las Vegas. I'm also getting a Smurf costume." She sprays cologne under one exquisite armpit, picks up her rug and trucks off down the hall for her last show. As I fold and pack away garter belts and stockings, I feel strangely old. I can't see myself as a dancing dried vine fruit.

Can't stand the sense of inadequacy this business exacerbates in me, constantly reopening the wound. Wish I looked more like someone's idea of a stripper. As it is, I feel like some creature under an evil spell—part stripper, part English professor's egghead daughter. What must be squirted on me to break it? Holy water? Coppertone tanning oil? Sperm?

Think I'll get my tits done. Dye my hair platinum. Get electrolysis all over my body. Tan till I'm toffee. Have my lips plumped. Never be seen without false eyelashes. And fake nails, the kind with little hearts or stars or zodiac signs painted on them. I'll read romances and heavy-metal magazines. Stop reading book reviews and scientific studies (about tan-beds, for example). Take up cigarettes and soap operas. Finally fulfil my lifelong dream to be somebody else.

It isn't just me. We're all running scared, leaping into tan-beds and surgeons' arms, smoking and drinking and snorting to take the edge off the blade that hovers over us, threatening to divide the beautiful from the worthless, the worthy from the nice tries. Will I ever become used to this life, lying around shabby hotel rooms, smoking and rubbing myself and leafing through magazines and writing to no one?

"Daryl lives in Brandon, Manitoba." Deanna, back from her last show, flops on the bed. She is still disappointed that Daryl hasn't called back but she can't stop talking about him. The way she sees it, he's her future. Her past is working at the Dairy Queen. "I can hardly wait till Sunday. I'm taking the bus to Fort Nelson. From there I'm flying to Edmonton, from Edmonton to Winnipeg, from Winnipeg to Brandon."

"How much is all this gonna cost?"

She giggled. "A lot. And I can only be with him the one night 'cause I'm doing the Regency in Edmonton on Monday." Her real name is Debbi. She and Daryl want six kids ("enough to form our own band," she grins) and they want a small farm. That one surprised me. I can't imagine all this unfolding seamlessly but maybe I'm just a cynic.

"Do you think Daryl can make enough money to support six kids?"

"Umm, probably. He's very talented. He's not making much money right now but I know he will, as soon as his talent gets recognized."

"What if the two of you are just starting out? You have, say, two or three little ones and Daryl is between bands or he's working in a band but not making all that much—I've heard that can happen," I say. "What would you do in that situation?"

She hardly pauses. "I'd just have to go back to work. I could take a night shift in town. I wouldn't throw out my costumes or anything." She gives a little laugh, edged underneath with something else.

"You're so lucky to be leaving," she says suddenly, and later, again. She is lying on her back after all the TV stations have gone off the air, her skin glowing like a lily in the darkened room. "I'm so lonely," she rasps in her low, hoarse voice. "So lonely."

"Have you always been?"

She raises herself on one elbow. She looks like the heroine in a women's magazine romance. Sweet, pure, and true. I wonder what it would be like to kiss her.

"Yes," she says. "We moved around a lot. My stepdad was in the armed forces. I'd make friends and lose them, over and over. Finally we settled in Grande Prairie. I quit school in Grade 8 and went to work at the Dairy Queen. I got to be assistant manager, too, but I hated it. The boss was this old fat guy, always grabbing my butt ..." Her voice fades out.

"You like this better?"

She laughs softly. "Sure. The pay's about a hundred times better." She lies back on the pillows. There is a long pause, during which I move closer to sleep. I've set the clock for 5 a.m. to catch the 6:15. "It's what I'm best at," she whispers.

"What?" I murmur sleepily. "Dancing?"

"No. Packing and unpacking."

Before I left I stood at the foot of her bed, inhaling sleep that rose from her in a perfumy vapour. I wish I could pray. Maybe on some cloud up there the patron saint of exotic dancers sits, a curling wand in one hand, a Greyhound schedule in the other. She accepts offerings of tattoos and tears; she blesses you with safe passage.

Called Vance last night.

"Great," he said. "Looking forward to seeing you. The house has a fireplace and the fridge is full. I'll pick you up at the depot." He's five hundred and twenty miles away, but there is more than that separating us. His voice is warm, cheerful. Hearing it, I think: somewhere, I have taken a wrong turn. Humiliation has become a way of life.

So anyway, here I am in the land of blue-veined sausage patties and pre-fab hash browns. Fuck. Just put ketchup on my pancakes. Have slept maybe six hours in the last forty-eight, including the last two, (curled around my mutilated Barbie). Dreamed a DJ was explaining "the new requirement" to me.

"Whenever one of your show times is marked with an

X, we want you to wriggle onto that." He pointed to a day-glo orange dildo fixed to one of the brass poles "and, you know, act like you like it." Woke up when the bus swerved to avoid hitting a deer, and Deanna was getting it from behind by a giant Smurf.

All flat from Dawson Creek, stands of jack pine and wild rose thicket clumped along marshy rivers. Saw a moose, just before it got too dark to see, around Pine Pass through the Rocky Mountains. Ranch-wife types with big pocketbooks keep glaring at me—must be the eye-liner. Have not slept except that little bit early this morning. Shakes getting worse. Mount Pleasant Women Object to Prostitutes—an abandoned newspaper on the depot floor. It's torn, and I'm too damned tired to go get it, but I can read, "... bad influence on my daughter." At Chetwyn a woman leaned down from the truck she was climbing into and spat on me. Adulthood is shaping up as I feared. It's just like fourth grade, only everyone is taller.

The bus is cold. I have been looking at a newspaper. The bodies of three strippers were found a few days ago, in garbage bags on one of the mountains that forms the backdrop to the city of Vancouver. Geologists recently tried to relocate a herd of twenty-four Rocky Mountain bighorn sheep. They knocked them out, put radio collars on them, and flew them to the Grand Tetons in Wyoming. Only two or three sheep awoke. The rest of them had died, it was thought from the shock of being handled.

I am crying, stupid me, hunched over the little metal sink in the chemical toilet. How lonely to wake up in an alien place, not knowing how you got there, and to feel the traces of strangers' hands all over your body.

They stood aside while fat bald Klein with his rubbery lips, Klein surrounded by henchmen and, K-Y'd and gloved in surgical latex—ultra-sheer like a condom—thrust his fingers up my five-year-old ass. Then the long tube with the light on the end of it, and the machine that looked and roared like your old Sunbeam mixmaster.

Just a little girl and already they tell you coolly, clinically, to put your head right down, raise your "behind," spread your "cheeks." My mother, wringing her hands—

hoping I won't remember this? But I do. My blood all over the room, spattering the chrome and tile. This, my dear, is how we heal sick children.

The gastroenterologist was Dr. Bergash. A tall man, who always wore a hat and looked enraged, he drew the curtains around my bed. Sometimes he ordered a nurse to remove my gown; if alone he just pulled it up over my face. (I scrunched it down, at least below my eyes. I wanted to see.)

He prodded my belly. Did not look at my face. Grunting, breathing hard. Flipped me over roughly to jab his latex finger up me, up my body that had "turned on itself."

My father liked Klein. He liked Bergash, too. My father had just rediscovered religion. Both men prayed with him at synagogue on Saturday mornings, no doubt thanking God that they were male.

Every year the powers that be released a new pack of students. The brightest of the bunch was allowed to devise a programme for me: fourteen little white pills, four big green shiny football-shaped ones, two flat round sharp-sided red ones, and one big brown bruiser—all three times a day, and no dairy products. Or: six little whites, twelve drops liquid rust, two green footballs, the brown bruiser and *lots* of dairy products, including a special shake four times a day. I retched at the smell of it. My body said no to food, especially institutional breakfasts: cream of greyish wheat; eggs boiled hard enough to bounce; oily, salty toast; bacon like bloody crusts of dried snot. My body said no to this crap. My body said, Leave me alone.

Dr. Lam was Bergash's new assistant.

"Get a nurse to get this thing off her," said Bergash. Dr. Lam looked in my eyes; he tilted his head to one side, seemed to ask my permission. Then he reached behind my neck (almost a caress, his hand brushing my hair aside), and pulled the string so my gown fell away. From then on, Bergash spoke curtly to him, as if he were a nurse.

Dr. Lam smelled like almond blossom. Once he came alone; beneath his fingers I became an object of reverence, a ceremonial doll. The gentleness of his touch shocked me. I was used to being handled like a broken toaster, a dented Chevrolet. I was unused to being treated as if I had feelings. As he palpated me, murmuring and looking at me soulfully, I felt the bitter ache of kindness, like blood returning to a frostbitten limb. I would rather not be reminded of what I cannot have.

Bergash had his knee on my thigh, pinning me down. Dr.

Lam was behind my head, holding my arms. I could feel his unease.

"Swallow. Swallow, damn you." The meaty, misshapen strawberry nose swimming in and out of focus. Gouty breath in my face and, worst of all, the hands shoving the tube up my nostril, down my throat. Blood pouring out of my nose and I'm coughing, gagging, kicking at Bergash. I score a hit with my foot and he presses the call button.

"Nurse. A restrainer here." (Like, "Waiter. More bread.")

The hard foreign object intrudes. I want it out. Take it out. Spit, puke and mucus down my front, my hoarseness falling all around us like … nothing. My voice counts for nothing.

When they finally got the nasal-gastric tube past my glottal valve, scraped down my esophagus into my stomach (green fluid bubbling out of the tube now), they left my hands tied for awhile, to remind me of their power. Leaving, Bergash leered, triumphant. The nurse was unreadable. Dr. Lam wouldn't meet my eyes.

In my dreams, year after year, I made a rope ladder from the sheets and escaped the ward with its white noise, its alcohol and Dettol smell, its blue-lit sleepers—escaped into the dark dripping rhododendrons, across the dew-slick lawn. Ahead the road washed pure by rain.

I still dream sometimes that I am running down 12th Avenue, past the smokestacks spewing pretty white clouds of burning offal against a bruise-coloured sky, my bare heels ringing on the concrete, my gown split open at the back. My shadow blooms in front of me, expanding like a bloodstain, then falls away to one side, expands and falls away as headlights slide by, caressing my back like the hands of absent people.

5:40 a.m.
Husky Station
Cache Creek (truckstop, population 100)

Up and down, up and down the winding road through these rolling foothills. Barely enough light to see but the guy next to me has been looking at porn mags—the kind where you can see electrical outlets and vaccination marks, like they were shot in somebody's basement. Whoever she is (was?), I only hope that was dampness mottling her paper skin.

Just got up to pace around. On the wall by the cash register, a "Missing" poster, paid for by the First Nations Tribal Council. That frightened smile. Shayla?

Dawn breaking over the Fraser River
Greyhound passing through Lytton

Dreamed of the tunnel under Deas Slough. Its red-lit walls streaked by me as I jogged through it in high heels and a hospital gown. Woke with my heart thudding, the cold stone of loneliness weighing down my tongue.

Friday, April 12
With Vance in Vancouver

The bus got in at 2 a.m. last night. I was ashen, but had put on lipstick ("My Flame") and the little, red wool pill-box hat that I bought at the ladies' auxiliary thrift shop in Golden. Stepping down, I saw that my hands looked greyish, almost transparent in the sulphurous light. A scrubbed-looking girl in a pink plush coat held a boom box and a teddy bear. At her feet, a rolled-up rug sticking out of the huge hockey duffel.

"Stripper?"

She nodded.

"Where to?"

"Just got in from doing Tony's in Trail. Have to be on-stage at Courtenay House at noon."

Just then Vance came striding down the platform, all billowing silk and flashing hazel eyes. Womens' heads turned to watch him pass. Swashbuckling, I thought.

That's the word. When he gallantly swept up my luggage I could feel the other dancer's loneliness pass through her bones like an X-ray.

He steered the Biscayne past empty, gold and green glass office towers. (Large painting in a foyer: a gaunt young man in a birdcage, gripping the wires and peering out through haunted eyes. "I like that one," Vance said. "He's charming, *n'est-ce pas?*") His citron and cinnamon scent surrounded me like fur. His voice like whiskey when you're half passed-out from cold. Teenagers huddling in the Cambie skytrain entrance. Lone woman hitchhiking just before the bridge looks straight into my eyes, a cigarette-burn gaze over a mouth like a fist. I felt as if we were floating above the dirty reality of the road.

He was murmuring ("That's right, mister. Swing it on out there, don't bother with a turn signal ..."), popping chocolate-covered espresso beans ("I really shouldn't, with my condition, but my doctor says my T-cell count is high and holding ...") That warm-throated chuckle.

When we got there, I found that he'd made a bed for me. The sheets were turned back. He said, "I thought you'd be tired." I was standing at the window—watery panes like in the house I grew up in—looking out through the thickening dark at snowdrops that had struggled up through the lawn. He has a way of waiting, deep-listening.

"You don't know how tired." And then somehow I was in his lap, croakily whispering about bus depots, and he

214

was stroking my hair. It got dark, and I could see us in the glass. He got up abruptly and came back with a couple of aspirin; I swallowed as he switched out the light. The moon loomed.

"'The moon has a strange look tonight. Has she not a strange look? She is like a mad woman, a mad woman who is seeking everywhere for lovers. She is naked too. She is quite naked.'"

"That's—"

"—Oscar Wilde's *Salome*." He left me then, and I scraped off my gear and fell asleep. But there is something about him that strikes a match in me. He knows, I know he knows, my secret, bookstore-browsing self.

Evening, Monday, April 15

Crying. I feel so alone. Which shouldn't surprise me—I *am* alone. Today I

read him my poems,

read to him from my journal,

was naked in front of him (bathing) for the first time.

He came in and stayed with me while I shaved the back of my pussy for tonight's shows at the Royal Towers in New Westminster. He watched, dispassionately, as if he were grocery shopping on a full stomach. I felt safe, and disappointed.

"Back in the seventies," he told me, scrubbing my back,

215

"I was one of three guys sleeping with this one woman. We all knew each other and there wasn't any of that possessiveness bullshit." I tried, unsuccessfully, to picture this happy, liberated woman tie-dying T-shirts and spray-painting Volkswagons. "When she got pregnant we all got together to choose which of us would be the father. It was based on inclination rather than genetic parentage. I knew right away it wasn't going to be me," he continued. "I've never wanted to be a father." People give warnings about themselves all the time.

Since the other night I keep trying to push the button on him where he is like other men, to make him respond to me like other men do, but I can't find it.

I have brought him gift after gift (silk boxer shorts; a knapsackful of organic Red Delicious from the high-priced health food store down the street from here on Commercial Drive; a tuberose, "to perfume your night thoughts"), and have failed to light anything more than a pale smouldering to match my own barely-contained conflagration. Have, in short, thrown myself at him, intoxicated by his presence, his voice, his feet. And he knows exactly how to tease me.

This morning he came up behind me in the kitchen, put his arms across my chest. My jaw strained to accommodate

the bone of his forearm gloriously jamming my mouth. Thrust his hips into the small of my back, taunting me with his low laugh when I ground my ass back to meet them.

("Oh, God," I moaned. "If you knew how my vulva—

"—I just love those little Swedish cars.")

Already drawing away, leaving me starved. I have moved beyond the pleasure of his company, to a kind of mounting despair. Never have I wished so strongly that I were male.

Wednesday, April 17

He was up the other night when I rolled in, rain-sodden and exhausted, at 1 a.m. from the Royal Towers, having spent the evening teasing off my G-string, S-L-O-W-L-Y, to the glazed, yearning men in gyney row. (I once saw one eat a cigarette at such a moment. He got down to the filter before he realized. I almost laughed when he gave it a look of horror.)

"I hope you like gunpowder tea," he said. "There's something magical about this time of night. I stay up for it when I can." Wind chimes, wind, the smell of burning birch. On the low table before him the teapot, two earthenware mugs, my *Playgirl*, which seemed to have migrated downstairs on its own, and a copy of *Sweet Bird of Youth*, which he's directing. ("Special effects for male strippers?

Just a sideline." He shrugged and gave an almost bitter laugh.) Also a collection of tiny nests and skulls—the people who own this house are field naturalists.

Leaning back, not looking at me, unfurling stories in his rich, radiant-heat voice. As he talked, I wondered if he was talking to me, or just an interchangeable unit of Adoring Female Audience.

"I suspected I was different in elementary school. I used to watch the blackboard monitor clap those striped felt erasers after school and I'd feel the back of my neck start to prickle and I wouldn't know why. Men were rough, crude, violent creatures. I already thought that, and it took me a long time to come to terms with my wanting them. I didn't come out till I'd been married six years. I was twenty-four. It's only the last couple of years that I've been able to have sex without being stoned out of my mind or plastered." He has stashed black vinyl bottles of lubricant all over the house.

I have stopped crying. I am pulling myself together.

It's not your sex I'm after. I mean, it is, but it's also ... I need you to come undone, or at least to stop looking vaguely past me and actually see me.

1 a.m. Thursday

This morning: watching Vance eat cherries from a big silver spoon. Still in my nightie, standing on tiptoe, mutely

begging (like a dog, and being excited by that) for the stone from his mouth. As he bent to me and rolled it from his tongue to mine, I felt the controlled recklessness of the fire-eater, the sword-swallower. But muffled, as if padded by the evidence, all around us, of homely reality: dishes in the sink, the cat dozing under a chair, drops of golden sunlight falling on the sweet potato vine trailing off the drainboard.

6:41 a.m. Friday

I lie here in the dark bedroom and suddenly the whole thing becomes clear to me, just for a second, the way a tangled garden on a rainy night can be suddenly explicated by lightning. Before I fell asleep last night I heard Vance moving around the house, singing bits from various musicals. Earlier, apropos of I don't recall what, he had recited some Browning. Something clicked, just now, and I saw my father, walking me around the Sunnyhill grounds, telling me the story of Ophelia.

Unfortunately this revelation—Freud 101—doesn't help me.

I am not what you want. Like a carousel horse that longs for the field, I am made of entirely the wrong stuff. Might as well be wood.

On-stage at the Royal Towers, I fix my eyes on each man in turn. I wet my middle fingertip and trail it along my cheekbone, my collarbone, my other hand undoing the ribbon at the back of my neck—a red ribbon, like the kind used to mark the necks of snuff film stars. I feel luscious and dangerous, in the dark lipstick that makes me look like I've been up all night like Salome, making passionate love to a severed head.

Late at night, draped in sequins and chains, I catch myself in the smoked glass mirror, undulating slowly, shimmering in jewelled gauze. My arms held high over my head, my long hands turning slowly in the air like birds, like fishes. I feel as if I have crossed some line, as if I am so out of control I am in control.

He was lying on the couch on his back. He had been talking, I listening; he fell silent. I moved closer, then stretched out on top of him, loving the warmth, the solidity of him. We lay there for a long time, kissing. I stroked his erection through his sweatpants. He fondled my breasts, then sucked on them. I pulled my panties down. He freed his cock, and I saw a drop of clear fluid at the tip. He stroked himself, gradually disappearing from me in the moment I'd thought we'd be closest. My desire vanished for good, a hot-looking flame proved brief and distant, like the light from a Roman candle.

"We've put the operation off for years," said the doctor, "because we didn't want to disfigure her, but eight years of treatment haven't touched her colitis. It's acute. If we cut it out of her, she'll be fixed. An ileostomy," he continued, "is a surgically-created opening in the abdominal wall through which body waste is involuntarily expelled. The colon is removed and the end of the remaining ileum brought through the abdominal wall and folded back on itself, like the neck of a turtleneck sweater, to form what's called a stoma, usually on the lower right side of the abdomen."

My older sister, Elspeth, had had the ileostomy a year before me, when she was fifteen, so after I woke up that horrible afternoon and looked down at the disgusting tomato-aspic lump of intestine, sitting like a polyp on my formerly smooth white skin, now marred by a ten-inch, dark red scar, intersecting lines of stitches giving it a centipede look, with drains and pieces of rubberized tape and orange disinfectant, impudently spewing shit, she was able to initiate me into the manifold mysteries of how to look after it.

"It" meaning the stoma.

"Some people give theirs a name," Gail, the enterostomal therapist, told me. "A man on East Eight calls his 'Alfred'." Those were bizarre days, and my sense of having been transported into a nightmare or, at best, a very strange dream, showed no sign of dissipating. During this period I attended a meeting of the U.O.A., or United Ostomy Association, across the street from the hospital. Several of the attendees wore bathrobes; some, like me, were accompanied by IV poles. Everyone was older than me; most were way older.

"Has anyone in this room been troubled by phantom rectum?" someone standing at the front of the room asked. I looked around at the tentative but finally quite large show of hands.

"Any minute now," I remember thinking. "Any minute I will realize this is all a dream."

In botany, a stoma is a leaf surface cell whose function is the exchange of gases with the environment. My sister and I would lock ourselves in the bathroom for cut-and-paste sessions, preparing new external bags, "appliances," for our stomas. In the middle of the night we'd lurch around the bathroom, laughing a little too hard, each with a pair of scissors. We kept two wet washcloths stuck to the edge of the round green sink, in case either of our stomas decided to spew. (It was impossible not to think of them as small, evil-spirited entities preying on our bodies, like fungus on a tree.) Sometimes we'd feel it coming, other times the shit would spew five feet. I felt we were a beautiful pair.

(Once, at 2 a.m. in the bus-stop cafeteria in Hope, on

the way to Williams Lake, one of the strippers I was sitting with accidentally spilled coke on top of her French
fries, which already had salt, ketchup and vinegar on
them. She made a face, looked at the rest of us and said,
"Isn't *that* sexy?")

Two shoe boxes, taken from behind a stack of rarely-
used sheets in the linen cupboard and placed on the
clothes hamper, were our source of materials: powders,
sprays, tapes, both micropore paper skin tape—which we
always, out of some sweet, vestigial vanity, bought in flesh
tone, never in white—and stiff, gluey, "waterproof" tape,
which buckled horribly on the few occasions I was persuaded to put on a swimsuit and venture into some
deserted public pool—so that water rushed under it and
broke the seal, leaving me with a pasty mess on my skin
and a disembodied plastic bag, rapidly engorging.

Karaya rings, made from the sap of an African tree,
sticky and rubbery and the colour of Coca-Cola, were for
placing around the stoma to get a "seal." You wanted to
get a good seal so the pouch would stay on as long as possible. Mine tended to come off on account of its poor
placement, which the surgeons blamed on my narrow
hips. Sometimes it came off at school and I would have
to run to the bathroom holding a lot of books in front
of me. I'd stuff the area with paper towels and sprint
home, ashamed and disgusted in my wet, stained clothes.

I had confided in some of the girls, who wanted to
know why I crackled when I moved. This in spite of

cheerful assurances in the U.O.A. literature that "the appliance is virtually undetectable." If such a thing is detectible, thirteen-year-olds will detect it. One day Graham Carter, the cutest boy in Grade 8, came up to me in the middle of Social Studies. He had soft-looking brown hair, a cleft chin, the face of a love-struck country music star. He had never approached me before and though I liked it (hoping he would ask me for a favour, some special task that only *I* could perform), my heart still pounded when he came over to me.

"Is it true you have a bag on your stomach?" Gradually, movement in the classroom stopped. Someone about to put up a map froze, pin in hand. Someone about to use the paper cutter paused, guillotine poised.

"*Gra*-yum," one of the girls whispered.

He turned to her, shrugging, saying, "Well, *she* told me," pointing to another girl, "and I was just wondering if it was true."

"They tease you because they like you," Mrs. Shapiro, the school counsellor, said. ("Douchebag," said the boys slyly when they passed you in the hall. Now they added a variation just for me.) And, "Don't take yourself so seriously."

Elspeth and I fitted a card with sized holes in it around our stomas to measure them. (It looked like one of those gadgets that tell you how much spaghetti to cook.) Mine was 7/8 of an inch. We used a hairdryer on the skin around the stoma so our skin was smooth and dry before the karaya ring went on. But still my pouch leaked. The skin on my stomach corroded from walking around too long with the acidic shit against it. At this point none of the "skin-prep" powders or aerosol sprays designed to create a smooth film would work. The pouch, reapplied, would once again slip off.

It was this cycle of poor seals that led me to beg for and receive, at fourteen, the internal ileostomy, which I have now. I was the youngest recipient. The surgeon uses the ileum to construct a continent reservoir inside the abdomen. The stoma is tiny and level with the skin. A one-way valve at the outlet of the reservoir keeps the shit from leaking out. The person inserts a blunt-ended rubber tube—a catheter—through the valve via the stoma to drain the reservoir.

My father came the day after the operation. It was the last time I saw him.

He sat uncomfortably in the vinyl armchair, holding his hat with both hands and looking for all the world like a man about to catch a train, wanting to know if I was "okay now?" I looked down at the battlefield my smooth white abdomen had become overnight.

"Why weren't you here?"

"It was Shabbat. It's forbidden to drive on the Sabbath."

"You could have walked."

He made a sound like a chuckle. "It was too far." I watched him carefully.

"The rabbi was here."

He cleared his throat. "I'm squeamish," he said softly. My shit burbled into a bag. So am I, I thought.

In the years that followed my father wrote me from Israel. His letters were flaky and tempting, like croissants in a magazine photograph. Written in fountain pen on the thinnest of onionskin papers. Descriptive prose from a man who loved his Wordsworth: "The jonquils are in full bloom on the Mount of Olives." Or, "The Jaffa oranges are a marvellous colour—a sort of crimson—against verdant foliage." (Yes, he would use the word "verdant.")

More and more, lately, I think about the young woman who drowned in the whale pool. Apart from my natural avidity (Did the water turn red? Did she really drown or did she die from punctures inflicted by those conical teeth? What did her corpse look like when they dragged it from the pool? Had the whales begun to eat it?), I wonder why they attacked.

I read in the paper that someone suggested their confinement in the small pool may have deranged them. (If only one could ask them, the way celebrity rapist-murderers are asked, "What drove you to it?")

"Whales are sonar animals," the theorist explained. "It's

as if you were to live in a house of mirrors, always having your vision reflected back at you, bombarding you with distortion. Why, it would drive you mad." Quite possibly, my view of the world *is* warped. My lens is warped, and all entering stimuli bends to fit it. Is this a result of confinement? Or alienation? (Endlessly probing cold corridors, alone, alone, alone.)

Friday night
Royal Towers

Backstage, Lynelle Lace, a pale, intelligent-looking twenty-eight-year-old with shoulder-length blond hair, puts makeup on her flat abdomen.

"I have these scars. See?" she tells the dressing room at large. "They're from Crohn's disease." I look at her more closely, recognizing the peculiar pallor of blood-loss anemia in her face, though her body is brown from the tanbed. Crohn's is the same as colitis, only it comes back, even when cut out. Looking at Lynelle Lace's three-inch horizontal scar, I feel as if I've met a sister who doesn't know we're related. If mine weren't so much worse, maybe I'd have her confidence, shed my robe under the relentless light and do the same.

Belinda Starr, the feature, announces three times in the course of the evening, that she feels like slashing her wrists. She then buys some of the Crohn's disease girl's painkillers ("Please? How many can you spare? What do you call that yellow one? Ooh, those pink ones are cute. Can I have one of them too?) and takes them in combinations, so that by the end of the night she is giggling, slipping into the shower stall with the DJ to smoke a joint.

I asked her what was wrong, why she felt like committing suicide.

"That's really sweet of you," she said. "I mean, you asked me that right away and you don't even know me."

The others ignored her when she talked that way. Daylynn said, "Aw, that's just the way she is." Belinda herself could only say, "I don't know why. No, I have no idea why." She seemed to avoid me after that, addressing her remarks mostly to Daylynn, a long-limbed woman a little older than me with a closed, watchful look and a lot of tattoos.

Wednesday Belinda bounced into the dressing room after a show and said, "What do you think of escort services? Think there's money in it?" I knew better than to volunteer my opinion but Daylynn paused from brushing her hair and looked over at her.

"I wouldn't try it," she said. "Good way to get killed." She's been stripping for five years.

Pulling out in the dark of late last night, I looked out the window of the taxi and saw Belinda through the plate glass window of the brightly-lit lobby. She was standing next to a silver-haired mid-fifties man in a grey three-piece suit. He was signing the register. If I could, I'd paint that scene, framed in the cream swag curtains, under the crystal chandelier: the well-dressed man, Belinda's face opaque and pale. Also, I'd had some sort of anxiety attack early in the evening, just after Daylynn whispered to me, "Keep your eye on that guy in gyney row, second from the left. He's out on parole."

"What?"

"Stabbed a stripper," she says shortly, then spins on her spikes and walks away. He was there all night, too, eating me up with his eyes right through my last show.

2 a.m., Tuesday, April 23

Got fired (or "let go," which means they paid me) from The Metrotown tonight because management wants girls with bigger breasts.

"We'll bring you back after Christmas when business is slower and we book the low-end girls," the DJ explained. "Don't take it personally." What could be more personal? I don't care. I got two encores and the guys loved me. Some stood on chairs, one law-student type loosening his tie, leaned forward like a man at the racetrack whose horse is about to win.

It's a bias of management. Whoever the guy is, he likes *big* ones. The wall inside the front door is papered with women licking their own breasts.

"And now," crowed the DJ, "a big hand for Darla Dubbledee." She turned to put on her robe and I, standing on the stairs at the edge of the stage, saw her close up for the first time. I can't remember the rest of her body— I don't think anybody ever noticed it.

I made the effort to raise my eyes. Above those unbearably heavy-looking breasts, she had a sweet, not particularly pretty face and, as I looked into her eyes with God knows what expression on my face, she gave me a smile, a sickening, touching, "Please like me" smile. Later, crossing the bar, I saw her on-stage. (A cartoon figure, a pair of parabolas with a woman attached.) The hockey game was being shown on a nearby screen. She did a somersault and crawled around on all fours.

I went up to a nice-looking man in a brown leather jacket and murmured, nodding toward Darla, "You think I should get that done? Is that what men like?" He looked me up and down quickly, appreciatively.

"No way. You'd regret it the rest of your life."

"But you must like it. You came to see her."

"No, I didn't." He jerked his thumb toward the screen. "I came for that." He cheered, just then, with most of the men in the room at some hockey move and I wandered off. I felt better, mollified. But I was aware of a spreading, submerged sadness, an algal blooming. For Darla Dubbledee, or for me? At the bottom of the pool we are the same.

The dressing room here at the Metrotown is a concrete warren in the basement, soundless except for a distant bass beat. The dayshift girls have gone home and Darla gets the feature's suite, upstairs. I wander from room to room, looking for lurking stranglers. (Don't know what I'd do if I found one.)

The edge of a hoop skirt is mashed in the door of a locker; an even mix of movie stars, housewives, and naked women are strewn across the ripped vinyl bench in front of the makeup mirror, initials carved and burned into it, a row of styrofoam heads are reflected in the fly-specked glass. Dribbling sinks. Tampon dispenser ("Fuck you, too!" the gouge rusted into the white enamel). By the phone, a mound of lipsticked butts, a torn red-lace G-string, and a bunch of agents' and girls' and taxi and pizza phone numbers in pencil, eyeliner, and sharp object.

In the last locker room I stop, meet my eyes in the mirror. I'm still me, and I'm still here. Besides, I suddenly notice, I'm gorgeous, scar or not. (Unlike Darla Dubbledee, I didn't pay to be mutilated; my scar is a mark of my survival.) My face, throat, chest are radiant with sweat. I look great in my white kneesocks and black spike heels, my white stretch lace undershirt rolled around my waist, my sparkling necklace. But it's *me*, not the costume.

I'm sitting on a bench, leaning against a row of lockers, my legs spread. I can see my whole self in the mirror. I pull out my nipples and pinch them till they're red. Fired or not, I am sweaty and courageous and proud, and they loved me. I put my hands down and touch myself, watching the beautiful woman touch herself. Breathe and moan into the echoing silence, and then come together, shuddering.

I've got half an hour before I have to start buckling myself into my removeable-cup, studded leather bodice and matching dog collar for my animal slave set. I'm writing, sitting with my knees drawn up on the ancient rotting brocade armchair wedged into this cramped triangular room behind the main dressing room. On the floor: an ostrich-feather boa (black shot with silver), a kicked-off pair of open-toed red spikes (mine), and—I've just noticed—a small, locked diary all but hidden under a cigarette pack, a lighter, a little plastic envelope of Glamourelle nails, and a delicate golden chain.

Silky Sins and Belinda Starr are dead, of a car crash and drug overdose, respectively. Mitzy DuPree, of ping-pong ball fame, is also dead, shot down in the lobby of the Sunset Hotel.

Lloyd is living with Fred's seventeen-year-old sister, God help her. I thought of sending her an anonymous note, *caveat emptor*, with a skull and crossbones underneath, or making a phonecall in which I'd breathe heavily and wheeze, "Get your own bank account" before hanging up. But hey, I don't even know her.

I haven't seen Vance since those three weeks I spent with him back in April. I stay away from him. It's not that I want to forget him, but why go out of your way to break your own heart, over and over?

I am doing my first correspondence course, "Introduction to Western Civilization." I wait until I'm in a coffee shop to open my returned assignments. It always excites me, that moment when I push away my empty bowl to open the envelope, with its "Learning for the People" logo, and read the comments written by a professor who's never seen me dressed, never mind naked, who praises my "insight," who feels I'm "astute."

Towards the end of the term I take a week off from the circuit and stay in a motel. I stay up nights drinking milkshakes and stringing paragraphs together on the manual Olivetti I got at a thrift shop in Fort McMurray. Along about dawn when I start wondering what's to become of me, I light a joint and smoke it slowly, staring out over the satellite dish, and sing cowboy songs until the sign over the coffee shop below me flickers on. I amble down, drown my hotcakes in syrup, eat at least one nitrite-laced pork product and go back to my room to sleep until afternoon. At the end of the week, when I mail off my assignments, I feel like when I was little and sent for the "Sea Monkeys" advertised at the back of a comic book. ("Teach them to do tricks! Their cheery agility will amaze you!" the ad promised.) They turned out to be microscopic.

"Brine shrimp," my eldest sister sneered. "How could you fall for that?" Everybody has to fall for something.

A July breeze stirs the awning of the Sunrise Market. I walk past it, leaving the Number 5 Orange behind me. I turn to head back at Oppenheimer Park with its resident population of old men in shirtsleeves. Gulls wheel and cry in the salt-and-diesel air. The mountains across Georgia Strait are blue in the distance—their snowy caps glow like white pasties under stage lights. Outside the St. Vincent de Paul Mission a woman shuffles in place. She is wearing a cotton housedress, thin as a hospital gown, the pale blue of skim milk. As I approach she turns her head. Her lips move—slowly at first, then more and more rapidly, but no sound comes out. Her eyes are a startling clear grey, almost lavender.

I step up to her. She puts her arms around my neck, the first slow movements of a waltz. I put a finger to her lips. When I take it away she is calmer. I put my strong, freckled arms around her stewing-hen ribcage and hold her, shuffling my feet, finding her rhythm, matching it.

I stay with her as long as I can. And then I am taking the creaky, wooden back stairs two at a time to the Number 5 Orange dressing room, so that when my music starts I will be ready to descend the brass ladder.